THE LIGHTNING THESAURUS.

A RON BRANDYWOOD CAPER.

ENCHANTED FOREST
PUBLISHING LTD.

Dedicated to Lil

First published 2021 by

ENCHANTED FOREST PUBLISHING LTD.
27 Old Gloucester Street,
London,
WC1N 3AX
United Kingdom

www.enchantedforestpublishingltd.com

Copyright © 2021 by Enchanted Forest
Publishing Ltd

A CIP catalogue record for this book is available
from the British Library.

ISBN 978-1-8383322-2-8

For more information, send an e-mail to:
enchantedforestpublishingltd@gmail.com

Cover art by Jerry Reid
www.ebookorprint.com/professional-
book-cover-design

1

Zephyrus ran through the night, calling the lightning until his head pounded with the effort of speaking it.

The thumping hooves of their horses and the joyous, terrified cries of men going to war. He had fled the grounds of Holme, the palatial estate where he rejected becoming a corpse buried in its soil.

Zephyrus Barak spoke and in the same breath, prayed for Ansel Mercer's men to give up their pursuit.

A sixty feet column of brilliant white and blue light sliced through the trees in a serpentine arc.

They knew this estate, eighty miles of good soil and spilled blood on the outskirts of Alsace, an agricultural ally to The Vivarian Empire, the ruling power for over sixty years. Holme was the castle of Ansel Mercer, a rich noble who had expressed a desire to meet with a scholar seeking alms. Zephyrus scarred it with the last of his power. Now, the lightning was silent, no matter how often he called.

He had shared his circumstances of birth with Mercer over dinner that same evening. Hatched from a divine egg; stolen from a dragon goddess, tricked into surrender by his father. Mercer had sputtered on his wine and sat back aghast. Zephyrus had expected the Principles of the Empire applied here.

Zephyrus remembered the statues of the major saints in the hallway.

The shard of diamond around his neck hung on a length of cord, a symbol of the Lord and her rebirth. He believed they were affectations, not beliefs held without shame. A faith, persistent and influential, but one which was being lost as Vivaria progressed and broadened after the ascension of Emperor Ignus.

Zephyrus put his hands up, sputtered something about being house trained. Such questions were common, more so seeing as he was six feet of blue-skinned half dragon, vestigial wings strapped and tail tucked away. He relied on his erudition and the papers of introduction from his instructors in Aldmera, which he carried with him.

Humour, he discovered, was another skill he lacked experience in. Mercer's face turned pale, then scarlet with an unspoken horror.

Mercer slashed at him with a dinner knife, screaming the word, 'abomination!'

Zephyrus realised he had been too honest about his circumstances. Taking a wound to his forearm had distracted him from the concentration he used to speak, so instead he had run, relying on surprise to make it out of the chamber, and then the courtyard before Mercer could act on his outrage.

Zephyrus remembered the papers he had left behind. A request that Mercer consider funding a modest expedition. He had planned to appeal to Mercers noblesse oblige, but then he had plans for many things.

Blood soaked through the sleeve of his robe and each step made it sing with pain. The wavering edges of his vision spoke to a blood loss which would overcome him faster than the men at his heels.

Ahead, the forest was growing thicker, and he continued his frenzied retreat as he heard arrows fly ahead.

Zephyrus prayed the assertions of a greater destiny were not his moment of ironic demise. An arrow slammed into his left shoulder. He fought the overwhelming urge to pass out as he tried to breathe through the pain.

Each breath was a furnace in his chest, and the lightning slipped from his acuity.

Zephyrus tried to keep up his pace, but his wounds stung with exhaustion and he fought against the growing lethargy.

Moira was gathering mushrooms when she saw the inexplicable flash of lightning, sudden enough to make her cry out with surprise. The sky turned an icy blue overhead, harsh enough to make her drop her basket and turn her head away.

She picked it up, plucking the few which had spilled and putting them into the basket. Her heart thumped in her chest as she wondered what had caused such a release of energies and why it was so close to her.

She heard his ragged breathing before she saw him. His appearance was enough to shock her from her considerations. Half-dragon, by the reptilian jaw and blue, scaled skin and dressed in simple grey robes, stained and torn by circumstance. She saw the bleeding wound on his forearm and clutched her basket to her chest.

'Please,' he said.

A plaintive yet restrained request offered upon sight of someone who was not trying to kill him. Such beings had always known pursuit and ostracism, and Moira was kind and nurturing to those who walked their own paths. Her own, for example, set her apart from most people because of her connection to the natural world. Such a distance, she believed, was useful to protect her people from harm wielded by the uncommon and unexpected. She had been a Midwife, but had left the order, whilst carrying their lessons through into the rest of her life.

His accent was unusual, but the emotions were sincere. Moira helped him. Mercer was no friend to her people, and he held the command of the largest army in the country.

'Come with me,' Moira said.

The sounds of pursuit, raised voices and the thump of hooves grew louder.

Moira reached out towards the being and offered her hand. He glanced at it, unsure of what to do, until she took his hand and looked into his eyes, dull with pain.

'Close your eyes,' she said.

His eyelids fluttered before he closed them.

Moira breathed in the world. The connections between all living things from the soil to the sky. Serene plant thoughts clashed with animal appetites as she reached into the web and tugged on the nearest connection. Zephyrus fought an unsettling change of pressure in his inner ear before he collapsed onto his knees, still holding the woman's hand.

The world wrapped itself around them.

It blossomed somewhere else.

2

When Zephyrus opened his eyes, they were outside a small, well-maintained cottage. Chickens pecked and scratched at the surrounding dirt, and for the first time, he could not hear the sounds of Mercer's men. He smiled, threads of blue electricity danced over and between his sharp teeth. It was a tremendous effort to do so, but he knew manners were important.

'Thank you,' he said.

Moira replied but Zephyrus fell forwards into the dirt with an exhausted enthusiasm, sent beyond her words by his injuries.

A warm, damp cloth grazed across his shoulder and the astringent smell of a fresh poultice reached his senses, rousing them by slight degrees.

Pain arose to push these fragile signs aside, and he cried out as she clipped the shaft and told him to remain still.

'What are you doing?' Zephyrus said.

The woman sighed and patted him on his uninjured shoulder.

'Helping. Return the favour by staying still and quiet,' she said.

Zephyrus started to ask why she wasn't using any language but then she did something to the arrow in his shoulder and it forced every scrap of thought from his head. He told himself he didn't scream.

She sighed and pressed a second poultice against the wound.

'One will staunch the bleeding and the other prevents disease,' she said.

Zephyrus fought tears as he felt the dance of lightning between his teeth.

'Have. You. No. Phrasing?' he said.

She came around and squatted in front of him.

Her eyes were a bright emerald, luminous with concern and focus as she wiped tears from his eyes.

'Some, but it's not needed here,' she said.

Zephyrus gritted his teeth together, his forehead knitting with frustration and pain as the astringents did their work.

'Says the human without an arrow through their shoulder,' he said.

Moira got up and sighed with a polite magnanimity as she wiped her fingers clean on her tunic.

'You'll heal, but may I give a word of warning to you?' she said.

He turned and looked over his shoulder at her.

'And please don't find me ungrateful, just...' he said.

He lowered his head and closed his eyes.

Moira knew the signs of pursuit, how it wore a person down. Her faith had burdened her with such experience. Distrust of knowledge was as common as dirt underneath the fingernails in these parts, and she knew distrust turned into animosity all too often.

'Who hunts you, sir?'

Zephyrus got to his feet, his flat, thick tail stiffening to serve as leverage as he turned to face her.

'Lord Mercer took offence to my existence,' he said.

Moira nodded, but the confusion didn't leave her delicate features.

'He's an adherent, for sure, but you're well dressed and eloquent, I don't understand.'

Zephyrus Barak adjusted his robes.

'I asked for funding. An expedition to recover a certain item which would be useful to the...erm, common good,' he said.

Moira went to the fireplace, picked up the tin kettle, hooked it by the handle over the flames and looked at him to continue.

'Such as?' she said.

He opened his hands and gestured towards her, imploring.

'The Lightning Thesaurus, once used to erm... cauterise the last infestation, around 50 years ago,' he said.

Moira grimaced as she busied herself with picking herbs to make tea.

'Such a thing would not offend an adherent, would it?'

Zephyrus, despite his distractions, caught her initial silence.

'You know of the book?' he said.

She shook her head.

'The last infestation, and what it took to defeat it.'

He took a longer look at her, gauging her appearance and complexion.

Pardon me, madam, but you look too young to have borne witness to such,' he said.

She gave a melancholic smile as she found a clay teapot and dropped in a few pinches of herbs.

'I wish I were, but my age is not subject to the ravages of time,' she said.

He walked towards her. A tugging sensation in the knitting flesh of his shoulder made his gorge rise, but he fought it.

'Then you know why such an item is best recovered over being left,' he said.

She took the kettle and poured water into the teapot. Zephyrus caught the sweet, yet sharp tang of a good blended tea.

'I do, but you went to beg for patronage, yet he tries to kill you instead,' she said.

She poured them a cup, each, made from the same clay as the teapot, and handed one to him. He thanked her as he took it, spilling some as his hands shook.

Moira gave him a sympathetic smile as she put her hands over his and looked into his eyes.

'What is your name?' she said.

'Zephyrus Barak, I am the child of destiny, set forth to bring justice and light to the...'

Moira chuckled and shook her head.

'Zephyrus is fine. And what do you want to do?' she said.

Zephyrus looked at the cup in his hands, closing his eyes as he considered.

'Not die. I mean, finding the book would be of immense value, but not dying feels more important,' he said.

Moira did not remove her hands from his. Her fingers glowed, callused at the fingertips and across her palm.

'Good, because I may have an idea on that,' she said.

He looked up at her with a tentative smile.

'Please, I'm desperate,' he said.

She grinned and patted the back of his hand, a gesture so maternal, Zephyrus fought the urge to sob.

'I know a man,' she said.

3

The gathered crowd laughed at Ron Brandywood, as he stood there, sleeves of his rough spun shirt rolled to his elbows, and his bare feet, dusted with curled brown hair, tracing a line in the dirt outside the inn. Three feet tall, in proportion, and far shorter than the half-orc stood across from him.

He grinned at Ron through a pair of yellowing, blunted tusks, his body swollen with muscle and tattooed with old scars. Filed down, Ron observed, which meant a degree of vanity uncommon to his kind.

Ron had his hands up, palms facing outward.

'Sir, offence is taken, not given, so why don't we come to something of an accord?' he said.

The man across from him grunted and spat a bolt of yellow phlegm at his feet. Ron looked at the globule in the dirt and sighed, before he raised his eyes to fix the man with a dismayed expression.

To those onlookers paying attention, it resembled an expression, though incongruous.

Pity.

'Now, sir, in my part of the world, such a gesture is an insult,' he said.

The man gave a rough chuckle. A ragged mix of cheerful laughter and indistinct murmurs of concern rose in the air. He clenched his hands into enormous fists, the knuckles protruding enough to turn the skin pale where they strained through.

'Sir, I did not get your name?' Ron said.

The man chuckled.

'Kadd Shield-Breaker, I'll carve it into your dwarf chest after,' he said.

Ron failed to keep the resigned amusement from his face.

'Mr Breaker, I'm not a dwarf. Simple mistake to make, but I'm a proud halfling, and such matters are important, are they not?' he said.

Kadd frowned.

'I'm still going to beat the blood out of you,' he said.

Ron nodded, as though Kadd offered some insight worth debating.

'Well, sir, it's like this,' he said.

Kadd went to speak, but before his words emerged, something in Ron's smile gave him pause.

A pause which came all too late.

The echoing impact of flesh in brutal collision, a brief paradiddle of multiple blows and the crack of breaking bone before they watched Kadd Shield-Breaker collapse and fall into the dirt. Ron stood there, shaking out his hands as though he had handled something hot. The crowd did not see the halfling move. A blur, perhaps, but nothing more.

Kadd rolled onto his back, expectorating a fine red mist as he coughed and one of his tusks hung by a thread of tissue, dangling from a jaw which had moved two inches to the left, sickening those onlookers paying attention to the incident. Kadd breathed in wheezing, grating gasps as he stared up at the sky.

Ron stepped with care and looked down at him, shaking his head.

'The difference, sir, and pardon the pun, but it's a small one, is I'm faster than any dwarf you'll meet,' he said.

Ron reached into the small pouch sewn into his canvas belt and took out a copper piece.

'Something towards your injuries, or a drink. There's no apology necessary, Mr Shield-Breaker, should I incline you to offer such a thing,' he said.

Ron looked at the crowd. They stepped back, all the mockery scoured from their expressions, and parted to allow him to amble back inside.

He saw a face he recognised and gave a nod of surprised delight.

'Ma'am, it is a genuine delight to see you,' he said.

Moira grinned and knelt to plant a chaste kiss on his stubbled cheek.

'Why is it when I see you, you're fighting in some fashion, Mr Brandywood?' she said.

Ron shrugged and took her hand, kissed it and gazed at her with warmth.

'Ma'am, that man requested to settle our differences in a time-honoured tradition. I obliged him,' he said.

Moira sighed and rolled her eyes.

'What differences?' she said.

'Why, the outcome of a fair game of cards, but Master Shield-Breaker sought to cheat us of said fairness,' he said.

Moira watched as people tried to move the injured man, who resisted their efforts, crying with pain at the simplest touch. She went to move towards him but stopped herself. She was not there for the cheat, but her instincts overrode her sense of the world.

'Are you working?' Moira said.

Ron shook his head as a curious light made his hazel eyes gleam.

'No, but I gather you might be about to change that,' he said.

Moira gestured to the inn.

'I might, Ron, I just might,' she said.

4

Zephyrus sat at a corner table, aware of the curious stares coming from every corner of the inn.

It was, after his recent tour to seek patronage, a step down from the accommodations he enjoyed, but the innkeeper paid him no more attention than necessary, so he could enjoy the simple pleasure of existing without fear of assault or capture.

He was struggling not to weep at this revelation, aided by the clean, cool goblet of water which he drank before hc saw Moira coming towards him.

With what he thought was a child.

'This, Zephyrus, is a friend of mine,' she said.

Zephyrus, fortified by the moment's peace, went to ask what help children provided but the child stepped forward and extended his hand in greeting.

Not a child, he realised.

A halfling. Dark brown hair in need of a barber, rakish and brushed away from a high forehead and neat eyebrows. The copper dusting of stubble on his cheeks and chin glinted in the afternoon light of the inn.

His eyes were a warm hazel, and his lips were parted to show even white teeth.

Zephyrus saw the faint smear of blood across the backs of the halfling's knuckles and took his hand with a polite trepidation.

'Ron Brandywood, at your service,' he said.

Zephyrus could not place the accent. A honeyed drawl.

'You've blood on your hand,' Zephyrus said.

Ron glanced at the smear and nodded.

'Not mine, sir, but thank you for the informed observation,' he said.

Zephyrus looked over him at Moira.

'You said you knew a man?' he said.

Moira frowned and nodded.

Ron chuckled and withdrew his hand, wiping the blood from his knuckles on his thigh.

'A halfling man, yes. Does that give you pause?' he said.

Zephyrus drew on his paucity of social intelligence and nodded.

'Not that I'm without gratitude,' he said.

Moira replaced the parchment inside her robes and shook her head. Ron turned and winked at her.

'Ah, the bigotry of low expectations forever gives me joy, Moira,' he said.

Zephyrus grimaced, waved his clawed hands in apology. Ron chuckled and shook his head.

'All in jest, sir, I'm used to such assumptions,' Ron said.

Moira joined them, sipping from a tankard as she sat down. She set the tankard down and dabbed at the thin moustache of foam on her upper lip.

'Ron is a good man, but a better bodyguard,' she said.

Zephyrus looked at her with a curious, tentative disbelief.

'They're both assertions proven only by time, which I don't have,' he said.

Ron leaned across the table. Zephyrus drew back, equal parts charmed and unnerved by the confidence on display.

'Who hunts you, sir?' Ron said.

Zephyrus swallowed as he leaned forwards.

'Lord Mercer, he took offence to my existence,' he said.

Ron held Zephyrus' gaze before he shut his eyes, considering the odds.

When he opened them, he gave a stiff smile.

'Do you have the coin to pay for my services?' he said.

Zephyrus had not decided whether this was an elaborate hoax at his expense or he was privy to a grand delusion.

'I'm not sure whether you're the man for this, Master Brandywood,' he said.

Ron nodded and got up to his feet. He reached into his quilted tunic and retrieved a sheaf of parchment.

'I was talking to Moira,' he said.

Zephyrus stared at her with confusion. With a flourish, she leaned over, whilst remaining seated and planted a kiss on Ron's stubbled cheek.

'Will that serve?' she said.

Ron lowered his eyes as blood rushed to his cheeks.

'Think it might, ma'am,' he said.

Moira looked at Zephyrus as she picked up the tankard and took a deep swallow.

Zephyrus sighed and sat back, folded his hands over one another in his lap.

'Is this some custom I'm unaware of?' Zephyrus said.

Ron gestured towards Moira.

'We've some history, Moira and I, which means you get my services at a deep discount,' he said.

Zephyrus Barak adjusted his robes and got to his feet.

'I won't be mocked, not when my life is threatened,' he said.

As he left, Moira stood and came around the table. She took his hand and squeezed his fingers in an imploring grip.

'Ron's kept me alive, more than once, Zephyrus. Does your pride matter more than that?' she said.

Zephyrus stopped and lowered his head.

'He's three feet tall, Moira, as a guide, a thief, I'm sure he's most capable,' he said.

Moira glanced at Ron, then back at Zephyrus. Zephyrus pulled his hand from Moira and left the inn. As he opened the door, he bumped into an incoming patron.

The incomer's chest.

'Where's the fucker who's hurt me, bruvva?'

His voice was a clotted rumble and Zephyrus backed away as he stared into the face of the half-orc, tusks sharpened into points and green eyes aglow with rage. The hilts of two short swords protruded at angles over his shoulders.

Zephyrus felt movement behind him and saw the briefest glimpse of Ron slipping past them.

'Kadd had relatives?' Ron said.

The half-orc turned, drawing a pair of pitted iron short swords before Zephyrus could speak. The edges gleamed, honed to a fine edge.

Ron stood outside, arms by his sides as he looked at the blades in the half-orc's hands.

'We had a fair fight, sir,' Ron said.

The half-orc wasted no time in speaking as he moved forwards, fast for his size. He swung the sword in his left hand in a downward arc whilst thrusting the sword in his right hand forwards.

Zephyrus prepared to watch Ron being cut down, but he saw Ron step towards his opponent, crouching as he turned his feet inwards and drew his hands back. His blank expression piqued Zephyrus' interest.

The blades found nothing but air, as Ron pivoted to his right and struck the half-orc in his midsection twice as he lifted his left foot and slammed it into the half-orc's right knee.

The percussion of breaking bone, and the flat, wet melody before the half-orc vomited into the dust as he staggered forwards, still holding onto the swords. Ron darted behind him, his hands a blur of activity as he threw a cavalcade of palm strikes into the small of his opponent's back. As abstruse as Zephyrus had found the halfling, he saw the awful clarity of his skill and realised Moira was right to have hired him.

Even though he appeared beyond Zephyrus' understanding.

The half-orc fell onto his front, the swords clattering to the ground as Zephyrus caught the whiff of sour vomit and blood. Ron stood and gave a pointed look at Zephyrus.

Without taking his eyes from him, Ron lifted his left foot and stamped on the back of the half-orc's skull. The grisly, wet sound brought a swift bolus of vomit to Zephyrus' throat. He turned and spat the taste from his mouth.

Ron shook out his hands as he walked up to Zephyrus.

'You're hired,' Zephyrus said.

Ron walked up and smiled at him, tucking his hands into his pockets.

'I should think so, sir,' he said.

They walked back into the inn, as Moira sighed and shook her head.

'Men are such children,' she said.

They sat down, ordered more ale and food. Ron studied his principal.

Zephyrus' nostrils twitched. The word, enthusiasm, translated into the words God Within, he had said.

'Which God?' Ron said.

Lowering his jaw, Zephyrus picked up his goblet and lapped water up with his black tongue. Sometimes arcs of electricity danced along his sharp, white teeth and blackened gums. Yet his smile was generous and there was a certainty about him which Ron respected.

'We exist in a world alongside them,' Zephyrus said.

Zephyrus did not like to mention his divine origin. The last such conversation had him running for his life.

'Monsters, too,' Ron said.

Ron got a leather pouch from his belt and fixed himself a cigarette with a pungent leaf, damp and rich to Zephyrus' nose. He found a small match and popped the end with his thumbnail as it burst into a flame. The smell of it drew looks of disdain but seeing as they had watched him cripple two half-orcs, they decided to be discreet about their disapproval.

'Intoxication clouds judgement,' Zephyrus said

Ron inhaled, his eyelids lowering for a moment as he took the smoke deep into his lungs.

He exhaled a plume of emerald smoke and passed the cigarette to Moira, who took a puff and coughed in harsh bursts, before swearing in a dialect Zephyrus believed to be Myconid.

'Part of me, Mr Barak, is always mindful of the situation I am in,' Ron said.

Zephyrus lowered his bowl and wiped his mouth with a silk handkerchief.

'You must understand, I'm being hunted by professionals,' he said.

Ron picked up his cup of water and drank.

'You're being guarded by one,' he said.

Zephyrus studied the halfling for a moment. His skills were obvious, but men at arms were commonplace.

'I appreciate the confidence, but even being here puts me at risk,' Zephyrus said.

Moira finished her ale and set it on the table.

'Then we should leave now,' she said.

Zephyrus stared at them both.

'I've not decided where I am going, other than in the general direction of away,' he said.

Ron gave him a surreptitious glance as he took another drag of his cigarette. He passed it back to Moira, but she waved it away.

'What else do you have to do here?' Ron said.

Zephyrus pushed out his chest and drew his shoulders back.

'I must find the Lightning Thesaurus,' he said.

Ron sat back and folded his arms.

'Sir, you're being hunted. A quest for a book isn't the best use of your time or mine,' he said.

Zephyrus raised his chin and looked down his maw at them.

'It is my...destiny,' he said.

Ron glanced at Moira, who shook her head.

'Is it your destiny to get caught and tortured?' Ron said.

Zephyrus inhaled and delicate arcs of blue lightning swam from his nostrils and up towards his eyes, which glowed an oceanic blue before they settled down into mere flesh.

'No, but… it would mean I need not return to this part of the world,' he said.

Ron took the cigarette from Moira and studied Zephyrus with caution.

'You said this was an expedition, which I presume to mean you know where it is?' he said.

Zephyrus swallowed with concern as he tapped his clawed fingers against the table.

'Erm...I know where it was last seen, if it matters,' he said.

Ron pursed his lips and shut his eyes.

'And where was it last seen?' he said.

Zephyrus grimaced, preparing to have his assertions questioned, if not outright mocked.

'The Ethereal College, in The Marrow Pass,' he said.

Ron whistled and shook his head.

'Your reach exceeds your grasp, sir,' he said.

Zephyrus chuckled, but the laughter died in his throat as he looked at Moira's expression of disbelief.

'You know why it's called the Marrow Pass?' Moira said.

Zephyrus had an amusing play on words come to his lips, but Ron and Moira were siblings in their mutual expression of antipathy.

He shook his head.

'Ignus sent three hundred soldiers there, and when they didn't return, his scouts found nothing of them but split bones,' Ron said.

Moira glanced at Ron before she spoke.

'Licked clean of the marrow,' she said.

Zephyrus raised his head, as though he were about to ask a question, but he shook his head like he was trying to dislodge something caught in his head.

'Is your quest worth more than your life?' Ron said.

Zephyrus closed his eyes and took in a deep breath.

'It... erm...has been foretold,' he said.

Ron's eyes narrowed to slits. A muscle fluttered in his jaw from the tension which sat there.

'Mine hasn't, nor Moira's,' he said.

Zephyrus frowned and stared at them.

'Then take me to the erm...pass, I'll make it from there.'

Ron gave a terse nod.

'Fine, it's your destiny,' he said.

Zephyrus sighed with polite relief.

'Thank you, my ways must seem obtuse to you, but they've gotten me this far,' he said.

Moira massaged her temples with her fingertips.

'Obtuse is one way to put it,' she said.

Ron put his hand out to Zephyrus, who took it. His long, clawed fingers folded over Ron's rough hand.

'To the Marrow Pass,' Ron said.

5

Zephyrus gave enough coin to hire three horses. Aware of Ron's height, he asked if Ron had any preference for a steed.

Ron refused, he was happy to ride with Zephyrus. His calm instruction promised the potential of insult if he dared to mention anything resembling a pony.

They bought old saddles, had the innkeeper bring them whatever he could spare from the inn.

The innkeeper, a nervous man with brittle blond hair and thin, chapped lips bought them a few loaves of bread, a wheel of cheese and some beef, along with a bottle of wine. He insisted on not charging them, which puzzled Zephyrus until Moira came to him.

'Ron has helped him in the past,' she said.

Recalling the mangled half orc left in the dirt, Zephyrus repressed a shudder, but Moira chuckled.

'He helped in the kitchen,' she said.

Zephyrus gave a wearied sigh and looked at her.

'It wasn't improbable he had earned tribute through threat, was it?'

Moira noted the peevishness in his voice and stepped back from him.

'What's troubling you, beyond Mercer?'

Zephyrus knotted his fingers together and lowered his head.

'This feels close to mockery,' he said.

He heard the sharp intake of breath and regretted his candour.

'You ungrateful shit,' she said.

He looked up, eyes damp with fear.

'Not you, Moira, nor Ron, but my gods, it is their mockery I feel,' he said.

Moira raked her hair away from her face and sighed.

'Welcome to the world, Zephyrus, they always mock us, for our dreams and hopes,' she said.

Zephyrus' nostrils flared.

'I have a destiny, and here I am, chased like a beast, when I came to gather patronage,' he said.

Moira folded her arms.

'You want sympathy, but I'm all about the tough love, and seeing as I kept you alive, and found a man to protect you, you'd be better praising me or Ron than lamenting that your destiny has proven to be difficult, ' she said.

She strode away, muttering under her breath as Zephyrus swallowed and realised he had proven the paucity of his social intelligence yet again.

Gods and monsters were easier to deal with than people, he thought as he walked to their horses, deciding to avoid saying anything else until they spoke to him.

He also vowed to decline answering anything about his reasons he wanted the book.

6

Podswark had gone after the half dragon with six men, and returned with himself and a squire, screaming and steaming from where the lightning had melted his chain mail in a few places. Podswark had watched the rest of the soldiers reduced to ashes by the abomination's magic. His solace was knowing he had struck the thing with an arrow before it had disappeared.

Mercer paced back and forth, rubbing the crystal kept around his neck between his thumb and forefinger as he muttered under his breath.

'We must find it. To think...'

Podswark saw an opportunity to deflect from his failure to retrieve the half dragon.

'My lord, he disguised himself,' he said.

Mercer glared at his captain. He noted the streaks of smoke, the reddened cheek and the quiet rattle of a man hiding his fear.

'Yes, he did, sir Podswark, and to do so, asking for money, at that,' he said.

Podswark lifted his chin and nodded, slow to hide the emptiness of his exhaustion.

'We... I mean, I lost men out there,' he said.

Mercer lowered his head and sighed.

Podswark waited for his lord to speak.

'See to your wounds, you...did what you could,' he said.

He watched Podswark leave, then instructed his guard to leave him alone.

Ansel Mercer shed the mask of nobility with a horrible relief, sighing as he fought the shudder of anticipation which came from his communion.

Stripping naked, he threw water on his chest and face, raked his hair from his face as he took off the crystal from around his neck. A wave of relief washed over him, as he sunk into the perennial weakness which he nursed like a cruel parent.

He went to the central brazier in the middle of his chamber and reached for a small paring knife, rusted with enthusiastic use. Ansel romanticised his sickness, saw the white scars on his forearms as proof of his devotion.

Away from here, playing a part he realised was torment spoke to the broken places in his heart. The left-hand route to power seldom demanded the best to its ranks. Ansel was no exception, radiating a need which drew things out of the dark, hungry for the chance to sit at the foot of power, then at its side.

In time, the seat itself.

Ansel, in his cups, considered this, but the results and the satisfaction he derived were motive enough.

He bled himself into the embers. Once they had been a maid's daughter, lured with a golden ball. The mother's screams made him insensible, holding his hand over his mouth as he wept with laughter.

A hiss went up and the smoke, blackened fats and the stink of bone stroked his soft palate, made him cough as he felt their cold, malevolent presence insinuate itself into his mind.

What is this?

The half dragon has escaped my men.

Such a sacrifice missed displeases us.

Ansel caught a tearing, haemorrhaging violation of what awaited him should their displeasure demand physical recreation.

His left arm went numb, and the right side of his face tingled like someone had slapped him.

The price he paid. Once inconsequential memories, but now they wanted the rare stuff.

When she smiled at him, as he entered a room. He felt it plucked from his head, sucked upon and then swallowed.

He does not remember her name. A faint association, lost to him without time to improve it.

We will send our worshippers. They are closer to us than you.

Ansel wept as a tight band of agony sunk into his temples as he staggered away from the brazier, gagging and feeling saliva drip from the right side of his mouth.

It would pass in time, but each time was longer in staying with him.

He collapsed onto his bed, rolled onto his side and hoped he would not choke.

Power twisted through him, made him slack and drooling. He was empty of everything but devotion and the pain which sustained it.

Ansel Mercer was never happier in his life.

If it ever allowed him to remember any.

7

The afternoon ebbed into a haze which demanded a lassitude none of them could afford to indulge.

Ron sat behind Zephyrus, who guided the reins with no more guidance than an occasional murmured instruction. Zephyrus prickled with unease, it pinched his lower back and stomach with cruel, practiced jabs of tension which made him breathe hard in the saddle.

'Thought we'd make a faster pace, being hunted and all,' Zephyrus said.

Ron tapped his left elbow, telling him to pick up the pace.

'It's easy for a horse to break a leg on an errant root here,' Ron said.

His singsong drawl made Zephyrus grit his teeth.

'It is for them, but look, if we're to get away, perhaps a little distance is a good place to begin?' he said.

Ron closed his eyes, contemplating, with a wry smile.

'Agreed, but we should choose such a place, not them,' he said.

Zephyrus' indignation made him gulp down air, as his fingers closed around the reins, but Ron put his hand up, waved him into silence and turned to look over his shoulder.

The wind through the trees, a susurrant rush of words but nothing else to rouse anyone's attention.

'Excuse me, would you?' Ron said.

He tumbled from the saddle, landed in a crouch which made a low, soft thump against the grass. He stood up, dusted himself down and, looking over his shoulder, winked at Zephyrus and Moira.

Ron walked towards the trees, raising his palms as he smiled like seeing an old friend.

'Sir, there is no need for such malfeasance this fine evening,' he said.

Moira flinched at the sound of the bolt firing. Little more than a sharp whisper. Ron stood there, hands up like it was all just a game in the dark to him. Gentle steps with his back straight and his head held up. A man who knew the way.

Ron's left hand darted up, then Moira and Zephyrus heard a choked cry from the trees.

Zephyrus raised his left hand, calculating the distance to include Ron's trajectory as he reached inside his mind to access the lightning. He asked it to spare Ron, but no one else. The air overhead sparkled like something being born but Moira reached out and touched his wrist, shook her head. She smiled, imploring and inquisitive.

'Let him do his job,' she said.

Ron watched as the man, face pitted with pox scars, staggered backwards, trying to reload his crossbow with a bolt in his shoulder. He wore boiled leathers, carried the thin musk of old sweat and fresh blood. He grimaced through a mouthful of yellowing teeth.

'How'd you move so quick?' he said.

Ron's smile fell away as he judged the distance between them, and what his options were with the man. Killing him would have sent a warning, but he believed in planting seeds of goodwill, no matter how stony the ground he planted them in.

'Practice, sir. Now let's do this as professionals, shall we?' he said.

Ron leapt forwards, palm striking him in the solar plexus and sternum as he felt the crunch of bone breaking against his palms. The man fell backwards, broken and wheezing.

'I've left you enough breath to warn the others. Mercer won't pay you what your life is worth to you,' he said.

Ron reached out, cuffed the man across his left cheek and then sat on his chest.

'I am a small gentleman, but I wager you're feeling every pound right now. So, talk or I will hurt you,' he said.

The man turned his head and spat.

'Mercer's paying good coin for him. Wants him alive for something, one of his men said,' he said.

He told him there were more out in the field. Some had stayed at the inn and ride out at dawn. Mercer had put a reward for Zephyrus Barak out to the guilds and agencies across Alsace. Those messages would reach people in days, and soon everyone would look for them.

Ron lifted his weight from the man, picked up the bow, cartoonish in his small hands. He cracked it over his knee without looking from the man. He kept the same, supercilious smile on his face.

'That'll do, sir, now let me ease your distress,' he said.

A cry of pain, then a gurgling rattle and a final thump of someone landing on the grass.

Ron strolled out, adjusting the cuffs of his shirt.

'Sorry about that,' he said.

He patted his pony as he looked up at Zephyrus and Moira.

'Y'all good?' he said.

They both nodded. Moira fought the urge to chuckle with glee. She had lived longer than she cared to admit and had expected to have lost her sense of wonder, but each day she found new ones.

The inherent humour of being hunted.

They rode on. Zephyrus looked into Ron's eyes.

'You're supposed to see them before they see us, Mr Brandywood,' he said.

Ron blinked.

'There could have been more. Lashing out at one snake is useless if it allows the others to bite you, sir,' he said.

Zephyrus fought the urge to say something. Moira was there, and he was going to be a gentleman about this matter. His destiny demanded it.

They did not stop as they rode on into the night.

8

Camp was a night in the branches of an amiable tree spirit. Moira could wake it, asking in her melodic whisper if they could shelter within its branches. It brought them together into a platform, dropping leaves to make a bed soft as any Zephyrus had known since the evening at Mercer's estate.

Ron sat with his legs crossed, eyes closed as he bought his palms together.

'I was harsh with you earlier, sir. It was not professional,' he said.

Zephyrus fought the boiling in the pit of his stomach as he looked into Ron's eyes.

'You need to explain to me,' Zephyrus said.

Ron ran his tongue over his lips.

'You are my principal. Your personal protection is my priority, so it involves remaining close to you,' he said.

Zephyrus frowned as he picked apart the baked tuber on the ground, steaming from where he had cast a cantrip onto it. Cooked

to perfection, although no one had any
butter.

'What about Moira? They hunt her too,' he
said.

Ron tilted his head to one side.

'She appointed you the principal. My say in
the decision was whether or not to take the
job,' he said.

Zephyrus reared back as he lifted his maw
with a cautious concern.

'What do you mean?' he said.

Ron lowered his palms to his knees.

'My contract is for you, not with you,' he
said.

Zephyrus was about to speak when he felt
Moira at their side.

'He's right, Zephyrus, Mr Brandywood is to
protect you, not me,' she said.

Zephyrus winced at the kind detachment in
her voice.

'So, he's bound to me?' Zephyrus said.

Moira nodded.

'You are too kind to consider your needs, Zephyrus. Destiny is not a flawless shield, and so sometimes it needs a layer of protection added to it,' she said.

Ron sat with his legs crossed, rolled a cigarette and lit it from a single match. He inhaled and nodded in agreement.

'Figured someone was following you, so it made sense to test things a little. Telling you, Zephyrus, would have made you act different, give off an air of trepidation, so to speak,' he said.

Zephyrus swallowed, his throat tight with embarrassment.

'I manage my emotions all too well, Mr Brandywood, it is my flesh which requires attention,' he said.

Ron smoked in silence, smiling as he considered Zephyrus' words.

'Agreed, I will adjust my approach,' he said.

The even tone irritated Zephyrus, the anxiety coiling in him like a snake ready to strike. His head hurt from the effort of holding his frame and he scratched symbols into the dirt with a claw.

'Thank you,' he said.

Ron and Moira chatted for a while, a dialect which Zephyrus had studied, but avoided joining in their conversation. He laid down, bought his knees up to his chest and let the low dance of flames take him down into sleep.

Moira ate an apple in small, neat bites. Ron enjoyed the gleam of juice on her chin and how the fire made it shine. Whatever feelings stirred, he kept to himself, settling for the gentle appreciation of beauty, unguarded.

Friends, he told himself, nothing more.

'So, what do you make of him?' she said.

Ron looked at Zephyrus, the robes which had lost their grandeur, a combination of hasty repair and time, turning the fine stitching and rich silks to a memory of pageantry.

'He's frightened, proud, thinks more than he says, not sure if he wants to be respected,' he said.

Moira chewed as she looked upwards, then nodded as she swallowed.

'I haven't seen his kind for a while, figured there wasn't a place in this world anymore,' she said.

Ron grinned as he rolled another smoke.

'I hope not, otherwise I'd be out of work,' he said.

They gave a soft laugh then lapsed into a comfortable silence. Glances, small ones shot across the distance, but neither of them gave attention to it.

'You'll never be out of work, Ron Brandywood,' she said.

Ron's cheeks flushed at the sound of his name, coming from her lips.

'Why, thank you, Midwife,' he said.

She grimaced and tossed the apple core, which he caught with one hand, lighting his cigarette with a match struck against his thumbnail.

'Don't, I've warned you before,' she said.

He smiled around his cigarette and put the apple core down.

'My Moira, such gestures are a sign of affection. A halfling laughs...'

Moira raised her chin as she gestured for the cigarette in his hand. He passed it to her.

'Easy and often, even at the worst times,' she said.

He watched her smoke. The feelings arose, nameless and potent, but Ron attended to them with a magnanimous focus. They passed, and he was himself again.

'Even at the worst times,' he said.

Moira took a long draw on the cigarette and then passed it to him. Her eyelids had lowered, and she laid down, looking at Ron as he smoked.

She ran her tongue across her lips, Ron saw the flutter of a muscle in her forehead, a sign she was about to speak. His heart thumped a little faster, but she smiled and wished him goodnight.

The whisper kept him occupied, but otherwise, he kept his watch until dawn, too full with emotion to find sleep.

Dawn had them on the road again, on the outskirts of Alsace, marked by the swaying fields of corn and the low, primal ordure of animal shit. The road was uneven, but the day exuded a zen calm, bright and cool. Zephyrus saw the cottage ahead and turned to Ron.

'Might we seek shelter? People should know their lord has turned to some form of malfeasance,' Zephyrus said.

Ron grimaced and shook his head.

'A good lord is as rare as hen's teeth, or they're made cruel by power, which is the same thing people expect in either taxes or prima noctua,' he said.

Zephyrus sighed, embarrassed at how juvenile Ron made him feel.

'Well, you are the bodyguard, Mr Brandywood,' he said.

They rode on, Zephyrus looked at the cottage with something close to longing. He craved respite but above all, he craved validation. The sight of himself in the eyes of others was a rare pleasure, it put fuel to his ambitions. Fear was seldom the reaction, once he had established the relative introversion and showed the attendant anxiety, but still he liked approval, or to have evidence of it.

They heard hooves ahead. Ron told Zephyrus and Moira to get off the road, and they took the horses down into the field, climbed off and waited for them to pass.

A trio of men, leather armour and rough spun cloaks. They rode hard and showered the trio with dust as they passed. Ron smiled at Zephyrus and put a hand out to rest on his forearm.

Zephyrus smiled back, to hide the terror which slid up his throat, anxieties heightened to a thin whine which drowned out everything.

Ron went first, then waved the others up with the horses.

'Did you see anything about them?' Moira said.

Ron folded his arms.

'Mercer's men,' he said.

Zephyrus went to his horse.

'What does it mean?' he said.

Ron came to the horse and scrabbled up the side, onto the saddle.

'Anyone with a desire for coin or a favour, who knows how to wield a sword, will be inclined to bring you to resume your conversation with Lord Mercer,' he said.

Zephyrus grabbed the reins and climbed into the saddle. Moira did the same, her face, tight and pale with concern.

'Where do we go? I know you've a mind to find the Ethereal College, Zephyrus, but luck is inconstant,' she said.

Zephyrus gripped the reins and lowered his head.

'I have to, because without it, I won't be able to-' he said.

His maw wrinkled with distaste as he took a deep breath.

'I can't use any phrasing, not since escaping Mercer the first time,' he said.

Moira and Ron looked at one another.

Moira recalled the air sparkling as Ron dealt with their pursuer and raised her hand.

'You've used it, you appeared before me, then when Ron went after -' she said.

Zephyrus shook his head.

Ron gazed at Zephyrus, a benign smile on his face.

'It doesn't matter, my job is to protect you,' he said.

Ron looked at Moira, then clapped his hands.

'Let's go,' he said.

They mounted and rode off. Zephyrus thought the action would soothe his nerves. Action, he believed, being a natural antidote to fear, but he shuddered as the reality of his situation stoked his fears to a new pitch.

Ron touched his elbow, told him he was doing great. The honeyed balm of his voice, cut with the urge of instruction, put him a little more at ease.

9

Look. The temple itself sat like a tumour in the Needle Mountains, covered in a thin film of lichen, pearlescent when the sun hit it, phosphorescent in the dark.

It was never silent. Not since the reign of Ignus' father, Harrod, had it not rung with the sounds of twisted pleasure and sacred pain.

A well-rehearsed symphony was how Mother Keeley put it, played by cosmic musicians of grave intention towards their audience.

She watched the child turn purple. Strangled by a prospective member to gain her notice.

She smiled and waited until the child grew slack underneath her father's hands then waved the man away.

He would do, she decided.

They swept away this moment of controlled clarity.

Her God held court without a care for the souls which fed it. Her stomach gurgled and her sinuses blazed with pain.

A cascade of fragments, emotions, sights and sounds. Underneath, the serpentine, chill commands slipped beneath rational thought. Agony and ecstasy had burnished Keeley into a perfect vessel for their will. It did not communicate in words.

All it had cost her was her soul.

When they left, she went to change her soiled robes and considered who to send after the half-dragon.

She smiled to herself, flushed with joy at being of service to her God.

10

The border to Alsace was another day's ride, so at dusk, Moira spoke to the trees and found them a safe spot to rest.

Zephyrus watched her as she stroked the trunk of an oak, whispering words which made his head swim to be in such proximity to an elder language. When she returned, smiling and pleased with the outcome, he found a surprising beauty there. The soul beneath, and the lens to collect its light, he thought as he led his horse through the trees.

Moira found wood, Ron built and lit the fire with a practiced economy. He got up, excused himself and gathered his share of the rations.

'The Marrow Pass is two days away. Another two to get through it without calling attention, if we are lucky,' he said.

The control Ron had, reassured Zephyrus. He watched Ron peel potatoes, the knife moving with as few strokes as possible, whilst Ron kept his attention on Zephyrus.

'What does it mean, to be lucky?' Zephyrus said.

Moira came back to the fire with a skin of water, which she passed to Zephyrus.

'The orcs don't find us,' she said.

Zephyrus sighed, struck by a sudden bolt of nerves.

'You understand, I've no other choice, without the means to speak the lightning, what am I?' he said.

Moira looked past him.

'Alive,' she said.

Ron put down his paring knife, tossed the spiral of potato skin into the fire.

'Without a purpose, a man may as well be dead,' he said.

Moira studied Ron with confusion, before she sat down.

'I've come this far, but don't think I won't question anything beyond keeping us alive,' she said.

Ron frowned as he reached for the tin pot behind him and passed it to her.

'Agreed, but let's eat first, then cut to the part of the dance where we decide to go on anyway, or you can leave,' he said.

Moira's eyes flared with hurt.

'Ron Brandywood, don't you speak to me like that,' she said.

Ron put the tin pot on the ground between them.

'Ma'am, frankness between us is something I treasure, but this is a pointless conversation,' he said.

Moira bit the inside of her cheek to control herself. She knelt down, glaring at Ron with a wounded disdain and then picked up the pot and walked away.

Zephyrus watched her walk into the trees. He considered the array of things he might say, but his tongue sat like a crippled slug in his mouth, too full with fear to move it.

Ron looked at the ground, then set the potatoes on the ground before the fire.

'My apologies, Mr Barak,' he said.

Zephyrus gave an embarrassed chuckle and put his palms up.

'I am aware of the imposition I cause, nature of the job, I suppose?' he said.

Ron smiled and sat down.

'Nature of the job,' he said.

Moira returned and set the pot on the ground. It brimmed with water, bronze and gold by the light of the fire. Her face was a taut mask of controlled anger.

'I'm not a coward,' she said.

Ron raised his eyebrows and turned to look up at her.

'It takes courage to admit fear, or concern, Moira. Yes, the most expedient move would be to escort Mr Barak out of Mercer's reach, but-' he said.

He looked at Zephyrus then back at Moira.

'If he cannot speak the lightning, then he is unarmed. To deny him the opportunity to regain such a thing, is to never have escorted him at all,' he said.

Moira studied the pair of them.

'That's a fair point. Power takes skill to gain, and keep,' she said.

She sighed and gestured to the pot.

'We'll head out in the morning?' she said.

Ron's relieved smile reassured Zephyrus. Both men nodded as Ron prepared the spit to hold the tin pot over the fire. They ate in terse silence.

Moira glared at them both but kept her own counsel. When she laid down and went to sleep, with a pointed sigh, Ron looked at her back and fought the weak impulse to offer reassurance to her.

Whatever his feelings, his work meant he had to be curt. With the principal, but also with anyone who presented tension or dissent. Everyone worked better if someone took the part of Father or Mother in these situations.

After they finished their food, the two men sat there, savouring the more companionable silence which went to sleep alongside Moira.

'How do you two know each other?' Zephyrus said.

Ron raised an eyebrow.

'Worked for her,' he said.

Zephyrus gave a low chuckle. Ron tilted his head to one side as he studied him with surprise.

'What?' he said.

Zephyrus narrowed his eyes.

'You're loquacious, is that how you pronounce it?' he said.

Ron nodded and told him to continue.

'Well, when you speak about Moira, you use fewer words. It's interesting, which was why I asked you,' he said.

Ron got out his fixings and made a cigarette. He lit it from the fire, and laid back down, with one arm underneath his head whilst he looked at the sky.

Zephyrus closed his eyes. Worms of electricity slid between his teeth as he fought the surge of anxious panic which infested him.

Ron sat up, eyes narrowed with concern. Zephyrus waved his attention away.

'Nervous condition,' he said.

Ron brushed the hair away from his eyes as he watched Zephyrus glow and flash, a storm condensed into a single being.

Zephyrus kept his maw shut, the light coming in bursts, aquamarine through his skull. Ron knew a few linguists in his time.

Some of them went out further into the study and practice of their language and did not return to their point of origin without being changed by it.

The problems of destiny, Ron thought, as he laid back down. Zephyrus would not ask any further.

'Moira said you're bound to me?' Zephyrus said.

Ron closed his eyes and took a centring breath.

'Yes, sir,' he said.

'So, does it give me command over you?' Zephyrus said.

Ron sat up.

'Not in this matter. However, you may ask me as one gentleman to another,' he said.

Zephyrus gestured towards Moira, raised an eyebrow and gave a nervous, furtive grin. His teeth glowed blue as the last worms of lightning faded away.

Ron looked at Moira, raked the hair back from his head and sighed.

'The answer is yes, but also no,' Ron said.

Zephyrus frowned and leaned forwards, curious and alert as an antidote to his anxieties.

'Why have you not?' he said.

Ron's mouth set into a thin line, his eyes luminous with pain before he laid back down.

'Right person. Wrong time,' he said.

Zephyrus sighed and shook his head. He laid down and looked up at the stars.

'It helps us if we don't become friends, Mr Barak,' Ron said.

There was an edge to his voice, a tightness at odds with the amiable tone of voice he used.

Zephyrus understood manners were a shield and realised he had been too curious for his own good.

At least Mr Brandywood hadn't attempted to murder him, Zephyrus thought.

It was a comforting thought until he realised Ron would not attempt to murder him. He would just do it.

11

They rode, hard and crazed, from the temple down into the valleys. Anyone who saw them, dusted in chalk, streaked with runic symbols and laughing at the chance to whet their blades for sport.

Skett-Al's knowledge led them to the border of Alsace. A few coins, a subtle knife in the ribs and they extended their reach by miles.

Whistling Grace rode out to Marrow Pass, set up with a brace of pigeons and her hunting bow. Her mastiff, Clot, ambled alongside her.

Edric and Skett-Al settled in. Their appetites were excessive, and part of their zealotry came from the explicit connection between the sanctioned release of them and the opportunities to find further refinement in their execution.

They stained the walls of their rooms with evil, and as the air hummed with their sins and malignancies, they sent out these offspring into the night air.

Searching.

Watching.

Waiting.

Whistling Grace invited herself into the homes of several families. She was quick, but thorough and she burned what she left behind. Sated and focused, she made it to the Marrow Pass, found a vantage point thirty feet up a cliff side where she had an unobstructed view of anyone taking the principal route out.

She amused herself by making up names and stories for the orcs she saw. Grace made it more challenging by giving them all the same names, and took the inevitable spasms of violence she observed, to be evidence of how awful her actions had been.

12

Moira was awake at dawn. She ached from the tension which wrapped around her as she closed her eyes and pretended to sleep. There were meditations which sufficed, allowing her to go into herself and rest. It was a relief to let go of the anger, left where it had no use, and weaker with separation.

The world deluded men like Zephyrus, to one degree or another. Their lives untethered in the way women were. Blood. Pain. Process. The connections and intuitions women held, which men were not privy to, made them less reckless.

Which had its uses, she decided.

Taking him out of reach was noble, but the Ethereal College was a place ruined by magic, and further despoiled by orcs who guarded it with a blind, brutish possessiveness.

She feared the Marrow Pass.

Lord Mercer had revealed his interest in Zephyrus, and with his resources, presented a genuine threat to their chances of success. Healing him had been one thing, but the continued obligation cut her sense of safety to the bone.

If the Lightning Thesaurus was even there.

Destiny was a dangerous burden to carry. For every Matu Sky-Breaker or Jiorghs Martindale, there was a Kiernan of Br'ir-Al-Asab to consider. She feared his quest, conducted on a whim, would get them all killed.

Or worse.

She would see them to the Marrow Pass, but no further, she decided.

They rode out at dawn. Moira held her own counsel, but she caught Ron's questioning expression just as they mounted up and she gave a polite smile.

'Everything ok?' he said.

She nodded.

'Yes, but I won't be coming through the Marrow Pass,' she said.

Zephyrus frowned, but averted his eyes from her. His hurried nod disappointed her.

'Well, that saddens me, but if you insist, then you are asking me to continue with the assignment?' Ron said.

His voice came close to breaking. Dust in the throat, perhaps, but his eyes shone with a quiet acceptance, not enough to keep the pain from them, however. She nodded and looked up at Zephyrus.

'You're in excellent hands, Zephyrus,' she said.

He looked up and lifted his hand to her.

'I wish things were different,' he said.

She took it, gave a dry, firm shake and then looked at Ron.

'You know where to find me,' she said.

Ron nodded as he looked at her.

'I'll see you soon,' he said.

She coughed, and looked at him, wiped her eyes with the tips of her fingers before she looked into his eyes. He gave a small nod, and she rode away.

He watched her ride off before he turned to Zephyrus.

'You'll be tempted to say something regarding this matter. Please, Mr Barak, resist that temptation with every fibre of your being,' he said.

Zephyrus took up the reins and led them out onto the path.

They had gone only a mile when they heard the thump of hooves, and someone shouting their name over and over.

Moira had returned. Her shouting was not from joy, but alarm.

The source of which, Ron noted, were a group of five men on horseback, axes in hand and one with the hilt of an enormous sword visible over his right shoulder as they hollered their will to power into the morning sky.

Ron told Zephyrus to turn and ride towards them. Zephyrus turned in his saddle.

'Aren't you supposed to keep me safe?' he said.

Ron glared at him and Zephyrus took up the reins.

'Levity is the soul of wit,' he said.

He mumbled it, anyway.

Zephyrus charged at them, desperate to have any phrasing available to him, but he practiced courage, and as he felt Ron stand up, and put a hand on his shoulder, he

74

wondered where all this irrational self-confidence came from, but it warmed his insides like phrasing and compelled him into action.

Ron waited until the men were a few feet away, before he told Zephyrus to keep riding and follow Moira after that.

'What are you going to do?' Zephyrus said.

Ron squeezed Zephyrus' shoulder.

'I have some skills,' he said.

He leapt across, caught the wrist in his hands as he swung his legs up and hooked them around his neck. Without pause, Ron pulled the wrist in over his shoulder and butted into the elbow joint from underneath. The arm bent in the wrong direction and the man roared with agony or tried to as Ron kept the blood from reaching his head in the leverage his position gave him.

Ron let go of the man's arm and punted forwards, toppling him as he grabbed onto the saddle and released him onto the ground, tumbling underneath the hooves of a fellow warrior.

Ron took the reins of the horse and turned it to his right.

He kept on his feet, with one hand on the reins and the other pointing ahead. Zephyrus watched him ducking to adjust his weight, before he leapt again, kicking away from the saddle as he reached out and grabbed the man's head in his hands and slammed his knees into his face. Ron landed as the man flipped sideways in his saddle.

Ron caught the edge of an axe on his left cheekbone. He bought his hand to his face and turned in the direction they threw it from. The hunter laughed as he reached for the crossbow on his hip.

Ron took the reins in one hand, pitched the horse right as the hunter raised his crossbow.

He plucked the bolt from the air and flicked his wrist. The hunter fell back, clutching his left cheek where the bolt had gone through at an angle.

Two men drew crossbows. Ron rode towards them. Following his eyes, Ron

realised he had seconds to react, if fate
showed any kindness. He leapt from the
saddle as the crossbow fired, and the horse
crumpled over its hooves, screaming in
shock. The sound hurt Ron's soul, but he
was already moving. The hunter charged
him, but Ron was already in the air again,
climbing up the horse and reaching out,
throwing rapid straight elbows into the
hunter's neck and face. Beneath the tips of
his elbows, he felt flesh split and bone chip
and the soft, rush of breath against his chin.
He moved past him. Bought his hands up
around his neck and twisted.

Then he watched the other hunter draw
closer, firing the crossbow as he roared with
fear and rage.

Ron caught it and sent it back, taking him in
the throat. He leapt onto the ground, and
watched the horses stagger around, riders
flopping or groaning in their saddles, if they
were not already on the ground.

He looked up as Zephyrus and Moira rode
towards him.

Moira got off the horse, knelt in front of him
and told him to lift his chin. She studied the

wound on his cheek. She reached into the pouches on her belt, took out a lozenge and popped it into her mouth before she spat the green mulch into her palm and smeared it on his cheek.

Ron grunted as the astringent herbs stung the wound, but he reached up and placed his palm on her forearm.

'Thank you, ma'am,' he said.

She smiled, blinking back tears.

'You've not left me a choice,' she said.

He shrugged his shoulders and patted her forearm.

'Didn't have long to adjust to the situation, mind you,' he said.

Moira sighed and shook her head.

'You amaze me how you don't know when to stop talking,' she said.

Her tone was almost admiring and Ron looked away, chuckling to himself as he walked to one horse and stopped it with a reassuring palm on its flank. The hunter was still in the saddle, rasping in feeble, broken cries as Ron reached up and heaved him off. He straddled the man, studied him and then stepped off.

'We need to go,' he said.

They rode hard into the rest of the day. Moira looked at Ron and he kept his gaze on the horizon, aside from directing Zephyrus on how best to ride the horse to their aims. She felt an absurd burst of gratitude as she kept pace with them. It did not assuage the fear, but it made it bearable.

The Marrow Pass was ahead.

13

Mercer laid in bed. His head throbbed and each swallow tasted of copper. Running his tongue along his teeth proved he had taken a good blow at some point. When he opened his eyes, the thin light of dawn mocked him as he sat up and groaned.

He called out, a metallic bark and a young serving boy came in, with a flagon and goblet, already pouring it for the lord.

Mercer snatched them both and poured from the flagon into his mouth.

'How long was I under?' he said.

The serving boy looked down.

'Two days,' he said.

How many, Mercer wondered. It didn't matter. Mercer told him to run a bath and have someone tell him what had transpired.

Mercer was not a stupid man. He was aware of losing about three days a month on average, but the frequency of episodes and their duration were growing. He would lapse into fugue states, return bloodied and exhausted, and yet things ran without him. These fell after communion or requests, and his power waxed even as his mind waned.

He needed the half-dragon. A sacrifice of such an individual would gain him further power, and in return, get some control back over his life again. These moments, collected and calm, were proof to him that his issues would be his downfall.

Freedom, power, all the ideas which came and fled whenever he connected to his

Gods. Their anathematic status was ridiculous to him, but he understood how those who controlled the culture of their nation, controlled its faith.

He washed from the bowl at the side of his bed. There were dark crusts of blood underneath his nails and bruising on his knuckles.

Looking at his reflection, he saw a livid bruise on his chin and a scratch down his right cheek. He hoped they hadn't suffered for his sins.

The door to his chamber opened. His men came in, ready to read off lists which showed all his works and pronouncements. They struggled to meet his eyes as they spoke. It was a quiet and polite gesture, which he appreciated.

These were good men, and he had resisted bringing them into his faith. His apothecaries dealt out many treatments for bad dreams.

So, Ansel Mercer listened and heard the unspoken arrangements loudest of all.

14

They carved the Marrow Pass from pink and white stone, large seams of it visible like scars atop thin, powdered soil.

Agriculture had been a lost cause, blamed on the ambient energies which leaked from the enthusiastic practices of the Ethereal College. Soon, the college was the only source of coin in the pass and the population dwindled down to just employees, students and faculty.

Orcs had come after a famine sent them south. The college, despite its wards and capabilities, had no stomach for the sudden, desperate brutality of the orcs. Attempts to retake it had fallen apart, and soon the Librarians rebuilt an additional seat of learning in the heart of Aldmera, aboard an Elvish city which appeared four times a year in the world.

Yet there were treasures and lore still in the walls of the college.

Thc Lightning Thesaurus being amongst them.

'How did you lose your phrasing?' Moira said.

Zephyrus looked up at the bloodied bones of the rocks and swallowed.

'I do not know. Mercer did not lay a curse upon me, cut my hand, and one of his men shot me with an arrow as you know,' he said.

She nodded and smiled at him.

'Look, I still feel getting you to safety is the best course, but if you don't have your phrasing, you're still a capable man, you know?' she said.

Zephyrus thanked her in a small, choked bark but he raised his chin.

'Without the lightning, I am deprived of my greatest weapon,' he said.

She nodded. Ron regarded her with a quiet smile, but still reached up and patted Zephyrus on the shoulder.

'Well, that's untrue, you've your mind,' Ron said.

Moira looked ahead.

'Will we be able to take the horses?' she said.

Ron looked past Zephyrus, narrowed his eyes and muttered to himself.

'Not if we want to get to the college without drawing too much attention,' he said.

Moira ran her tongue over her lips.

'Any attention is too much,' she said.

Ron directed them to a small copse of trees, wilting in the shadow and they dismounted, taking off whatever supplies they had and distributed them amongst themselves. Ron slapped each horse on the rump and sent them on their way. They might make it, he thought, but then so might we.

Ron turned to the pair of them.

'Now, this is how it goes. I am on point which means you keep a distance from me. I watch out for anything, but unless I come to you, then you observe that distance, understand me?' he said.

They both nodded.

'The aim here is to avoid the orcs at all possible. We all know what they're capable of,' he said.

Zephyrus nodded as his heart thumped against his ribs.

'Once we're in the college, I can find the Thesaurus, I swear it,' he said.

Moira grimaced at the earnest notes of naivete in his voice.

'Hope is a lovely thing, Zephyrus, but let's not make it the basis of this, shall we?' she said.

Ron sighed and looked at her.

'You're both right,' he said.

A breeze betrayed them. Ron's baritone, a syllable echoed and reached the ear of a pair of young orc warriors, grappling with one another to burn off the constant stream of feeling which they drowned within.

They stopped, looked at one another and burst into laughter. Grabbing weapons, they ran out of the cave, looked down at the entrance to the pass through the curtain of powdered hair which covered the entrance and called back to the others.

Ron heard the cries from overhead and turned around.

'Well, we had the idea of being hidden from them,' he said.

Moira and Zephyrus reached for one another in their mutual shock.

'What do we do?' Zephyrus said.

Ron did not look back as he watched the curtain over the cave twist and lift as a pair of orcs came charging towards them.

And another trio after that.

'Run,' Ron said.

He did not join them. The first pair unsheathed swords from over their backs, all the while, sprinting to meet him.

The orc charged at them, sword held overhead as it roared at them, tusks gleaming with pink spit.

Ron snapped out the instep of his left foot across the distance, like he was dipping his toe into a bath to test how hot the water was. Moira turned away at the sickening volume of the snap where the orc's knee broke in the opposite direction of the blow.

The orc buckled as the sword slipped from his palm and as its head flopped back, Ron snapped out the fingers of his right hand, stiffened like blades as they sunk into the soft flesh beneath the orcs chin.

Zephyrus shuddered as Ron flicked black blood from his fingers.

Ron wiggled his toes as the second orc came towards him. Ron jumped, tucking his knees up to his chest as his arms stretched out, reaching behind the back of the orc's head as he embraced him like he was family.

They designed the Eastern Rolling Embrace as a diversion, the hands positioned to stun the incoming opponent, but the orcs were unsparing and unreasonable. They would kill or die. It was, to them, an honour to die in combat. A broken neck later, the orc went on to whatever came afterwards.

Two Irrational Elbows and a Fierce Joke put paid to the others. Ron looked irritated until he stopped and put his hand out.

'Forgive me, if I appear to be a man of violence, sir,' he said.

Zephyrus reached his hand out, offering his handkerchief.

'Forgive you? I welcome it,' he said.

Ron sighed and shook his head.

'Shame, there was a perfect moment and my hope was to sit and hope it comes to me again.' he said.

He looked at Zephyrus.

'They're persistent,' he said.

Zephyrus shook his head.

'It saddens me to see such a site of tremendous significance polluted by such barbarism,' he said.

Ron gave a terse nod and returned to Zephyrus and Moira.

'Yes, sir,' he said.

Moira looked up at the ruins of the valley, the palsied white bark.

'Ansel Mercer hasn't forgotten you, Zephyrus, and you still want to go find -'

She sucked in a breath, like they wounded her. Zephyrus went to ask if they injured her, but Ron took a step towards them and shook his head, trusting Zephyrus to catch his look.

'There's no time for this, sir,' Ron said.

They stopped and looked at one another.

Moira wiped her eyes and nodded, gathering her things without looking at either of them.

'Sir how close to the book, are we?'

Zephyrus coughed and blue lightning flashed between his teeth.

'The last known location of the book,' she said

Ron glanced at Moira, a bolus of concern seething in his stomach.

'Is the book there?' he said.

Zephyrus frowned and clapped his hands.

'Last known location,' he said.

Ron shut his eyes, let the feeling pass like searching for the perfect spot to release a kite or catch a fish.

'Then we are heading there?' Ron said.

Zephyrus looked between them and then turned away, picked up his bag and slung it around his shoulder.

'I see no other choice,' Zephyrus said.

15

He awoke to the hope of the half-dragon being returned to him, unspoiled and ready for his hungry Gods. The cult were most effective, despite their ideological adherence to excess, but it saved more of his men facing death or injury, and then questions which might reach the ears of other interested parties.

If the half-dragon hadn't left the region already. Despite the power within him, Zephyrus had been meek, nervous for such a bold countenance. His constant hum of power had awoken the parts of Mercer wired for faith to where the knife was in his hand before he could stop himself.

He escaped however, and Mercer's frustration was clouding his judgement.

Patience, he told himself, was a virtue of the noble. It was easier to show, than to accept. His insides ached with the constant tension of keeping it all in, not knowing whether success was coming or a greater failure. These pressures warped him in some fashion, and even the rest or release he granted himself grew thinner, despite the excesses.

Mercer could not be alone in a room with himself, and it was a skill he needed more than ever.

He focused on the men he had out there, both his own and those of his Faith. Another day, or two, and then Zephyrus could be his. With his death, would come enough power to grant him peace.

Power, first then peace to follow.

However, he sent word to have his horses saddled and shoed, and for his sword. Part of him was itching to get out there, the risk itself itched like a need, but he waited for reports and sat with the risk, savouring it like a wonderful new means to destroy himself.

Edric and Sket-Al rode for the Marrow Pass. They had awoken in the night, heads aching and guts bubbling with the need to hunt. Their faithful had developed instincts to better serve their will. Despite unsettled bills and unmade beds, the innkeeper was glad of their custom, and alive to enjoy it.

Stolen horses took them from the border, and they rode to meet Whispering Grace.

Edric spat onto the earth as he sent the horse on its way. He smiled at the blood-stained rocks and adjusted the sword on his left hip.

'Good ground to fight them on, eh?' he said.

Sket-Al squatted and lifted the powdered soil to his nostrils.

'Grace will know where the orcs are, it's the half dragon who is our business. He has to be kept alive,' he said.

Edric sighed and walked over to his companion.

'I know how to cut someone so they'll live, but they will suffer for it,' he said.

Sket-Al got to his feet, picking up the longbow and quiver which had sat to one side like a loyal pet.

'Pain is a welcome gift, Edric, now let us go and deliver it,' he said.

They moved into the valley, even their shadows seethed with violent intention as they went to find their third.

Whispering Grace had made herself a platform, gathering what few branches were around to form a base in an overhanging Scythe tree, hidden by the blossoms. Orcs had died to amuse her, but she could move and set up without being seen. They fought one another for entertainment, so a lone wandering orc made a fine and convenient target. She had killed six by the time Edric and Skett-Al found her and had her eye on a pregnant female before they disturbed her contemplation. She smiled to see them, because they promised action and the ultimate test of their faith.

Horror. They bought horror as an act of devotion.

16

Ron crept through the rocks, instructing the others to stop whenever he did. He moved with care, careful to keep quiet even as the air of the valley echoed with the roars and screams of the orcs at play, muted by distance.

He glanced over his shoulder at Zephyrus and Moira and smiled at them. Their attempts were unconvincing, but it satisfied Ron and he returned to his duties. He waited for them to join him.

'Do you know where the college is?' Moira said.

Zephyrus nodded as he plucked the sodden material of his tunic away from his chest.

'Yes, you cannot miss it,' he said.

Moira grimaced and looked at him with a withheld tolerance.

'If only we could, Zephyrus. If only,' she said.

Zephyrus drew his lips back over his teeth.

'You're here, Moira, which I appreciate, but just maybe you could not enjoy this so much?' he said.

She raised an eyebrow as a sharp spike of indignation struck her through her stomach.

'What do you mean? I came back to you, when there was cause...' she said.

Zephyrus looked up.

'I'm sure you've forged a fine string of reasons, as have I. However, your inconsistency upsets Mr Brandywood, and as he works better when he's not in such a state, I would appreciate you offering help or silence,' he said.

Moira gritted her teeth and clenched her hands into fists.

'I took the fucking arrow from your back, you petulant shit,' she said.

She kept the volume from her voice, but not the emotion beneath it.

Zephyrus squared his upper body.

'Moira, this isn't the time...' he said.

She shook her head and pointed at him.

'No, that time was when you collapsed in my garden, begging for help,' she said.

Zephyrus lifted his chin and blinked the dust from his eyes.

'Yet you stayed to help, Moira. I appreciate it more than you know, even if I don't know how to say it,' he said.

She stared at him. His eyes were damp, and again, she saw in his countenance, someone bearing a burden too large to manage alone. It endeared her to him, not because of the size of it, but the fact he bore it at all with any confidence.

'Thank you,' she said.

'You don't owe me anything, Moira, but I appreciate you being here,' he said.

She stepped forwards, put out her hand and touched his face. He turned his face to rest in her hand.

'Thank you,' he said.

Ron gave a soft cough.

'This is delightful, but we need to keep moving,' he said.

Zephyrus felt the blood rush to his cheeks as he stepped back from Moira. She turned and leaned forwards to look Ron in the eyes.

'Clearing the air, which is something you and I ought to do at some point, agreed?' she said.

He frowned and gave a brief nod before he turned back and continued along the winding path.

Zephyrus watched him before he looked at Moira and gestured down the path.

'Shall we indulge my mania once again?' he said.

She chuckled and shook her head.

'Don't push it,' she said.

17

Language generated a tremendous amount of power.

It permeated the world through repetition and intention. The ruins of The Ethereal College sang with the ghosts of a hundred thousand phrases.

Zephyrus tasted it in the back of his throat. The cool mineral wash of ozone. Moira's abdomen throbbed and her upper arms prickled with tension.

Ron stopped to look at them. He raised an eyebrow.

'We must be close,' he said.

Ron smiled and turned back as he dropped into a crouch and raised his hand for them to stop. Talking. Moving. Anything.

The low coarse rumbling of orcs. Ron had learned a few phrases, insults aimed at him, so it was a specific area of dialect.

They were belittling one another. Without an external focus, they fell into aggressive insult and conflict. Ron hoped it would blind them to their passage.

The three travellers stood still until Ron waved at them to follow him. Zephyrus remembered to breathe, clearing the black spots from his eyes as he staggered forwards.

Moira reached into her robes and found a square of cloth, slipped it over her head to keep her hair back from her face. She retrieved a dagger from the sleeve of her robe and nodded to Zephyrus.

'Let's find your college,' she said.

Zephyrus smiled at her as Ron led them with care along a winding path, fringed by horned bushes so they trusted the natural coverage and distraction. Ron stopped, kneeled down and took up a pinch of dirt between his fingers, flicked it into the air and studied the direction before he brushed his hands and grinned at them.

'This way,' he said.

The path went upwards, deprived them of the bushes but Ron saw no movement and kept their pace until they headed down into a crevasse, thick with shadows and tangled, palsied roots.

What life there was, altered by the exposure to magic.

The thin hum of insects grew as they kept moving. It was dark when they stopped for the evening. Moira reached out to a wizened tree, rested her fingers against its trunk and coaxed it into service. When she finished, and the branches reached overhead, the splintering white flesh became visible as the bark split, she turned and spat onto the ground.

She looked at Zephyrus.

'What on earth did they do here?' she said.

Zephyrus put his hands up.

'All before my time. They studied and practiced Phrasing in all the languages,' he said.

She wiped her mouth with the back of her hand and exhaled to cool the sweat gathered on her brow.

'If you knew what the trees did, you'd run screaming from this place,' she said.

Ron turned, darted towards them as he put his hands up, waving to attract their attention.

The roar shook the surrounding air. Hoots of alarm and pleasure at the alarm.

Three orcs ran towards them, knives in hand. Ron saw the ropes of saliva swinging from their tusks and the dull porcine light in their eyes.

Behind him, Ron registered the sound of more arrivals. Moira cried out and Zephyrus whimpered as the orcs plunged towards them.

Zephyrus flexed his fingers as claws slid forwards from vertical slashes in the tips.

His lips drew back over his teeth as he hissed with fear and fury.

Ron ran towards Zephyrus, stepped in front of him to kick the orc in his right hip and send him spinning. Ron stayed with the orc as he fell, swinging elbows into the centre of his face, focused on the nose and the orbital bones. Blind or struggling to breathe, either way Ron wanted to take them out of the fight, rather than the world.

Dead orcs told no tales, but living cripples got the word out.

Bone splintered and caved beneath the skin as the orc gargled and grunted, breathing through a mouthful of blood before he hit the ground. Ron was already off him, closing the distance to the orc in the middle.

He dropped into a squat, punched into the small of the orc's back as he passed. A tight quartet of rapid jabs which lit up the orcs nervous system like a torch. As he turned, Ron drove his elbow into the spot where his liver was. The resulting blow allowed the orc a few more steps before he collapsed to the ground.

Moira had the knife out before Ron could reach her. She stabbed upwards, and Ron gave a small, awkward smile as he watched her apply his teaching to her benefit.

The blade flicked forwards, like a snake. Under the arm, twist then out, groin or throat, whatever is closest. Twist as you pulled out the blade. You didn't stab to cut or parry, you did it to deter the adventurous, as Ron put it. A pleasant phrase to sit atop a series of ugly intentions. Death. Survival.

The orc rolled onto his side, clutching his armpit with one hand as he pressed his palm to his open throat, spraying a fine mist of blood as he choked and bled out. He looked up at Ron with disbelief before he fell onto his back, dying.

Ron turned and stepped in front of Moira. He had no time to see: trusting his instincts as he threw out knee strikes, aiming for the thighs of the orc as he blocked the incoming knife blows with his forearms.

The blade sliced through the leather of his coat and Ron gasped as he drove his knee into the thigh of the orc.

An artery in the thigh, if struck with enough force, induced shock.

If you did it twice, you could kill someone with it.

Ron did it twice to make sure. He pushed into the orc's midsection, blood pouring down his forearm as he drove a straight punch under the orc's chin. Ron kept his wounded arm close to his chest as the orc fell backwards.

Ron stayed with him, letting his momentum do several unpleasant things to the orc's ribs and lungs. A forced introduction which drove a pink froth to the lips of the orc. He died with a rattle in his throat, but Ron was already up by then.

He tried to speak but his head was light, and the words escaped him. Bursts of white kept exploding before his eyes and his feet refused to move.

Someone caught him, he thought, as he fell backwards, letting go of everything except the bright light engulfing him.

Down to his finest, final thought.

18

Whispering Grace followed the orcs. Framed against the bow, she studied their behaviour, although she gave them all the same names out of contempt.

Their outbursts were opportunities to witness violence.

They ate, slept and bred with the same vigour.

Violence inspired the most enthusiasm from them.

Edric and Skett-Al were asleep, having watched through the night but Grace enjoyed the afternoons when the pass was quiet. She savoured silence, it allowed the privacy of her own thoughts and meant she was free of any fears beyond those invested in her Gods.

Grace, with her bow and arrows, had been a simple man's wife and a dead child's mother before she listened to the promise of a better life than what remained to her.

Years of repressed violence and frustration found an outlet in the cult, and Grace, who

could not read nor write, became eloquent
in another art form altogether.

Those who laughed when she would
volunteer found little amusement in her skill:
Only envy then awe at the horror for anyone
who crossed her path.

Her chosen weapon was the bow.

She saw the orcs, young and enthusiastic,
stop and look down into the crevasse,
pointing and gesturing downwards, in
silence.

Grace moved from her vantage point,
climbing higher into the branches of the tree
and then forwards, kneeling to provide a
better firing position.

The fight, when it came, was sudden and
impressive. A boy, she believed, fighting
orcs without a weapon in his hands,
amused her. He leapt and grappled
between them, without theatrics beyond
boldness and a willingness to put one's
body to work.

No boy at all, she realised, when he stood up, dusting himself down as he spoke to his companions.

The half-dragon, a woman and a halfling.

With shaking hands, she drew the string back, cocked the arrow and adjusted for the wind and distance. Her body hummed with focus as she held in a breath, aiming for the centre of his mass. The halfling moved too fast to wear much in armour and so Whispering Grace shot the halfling in the chest.

As he fell, Grace was already climbing down, calling her companions to share in her good fortune. They were to keep the half dragon alive, but the others were sport, and so their excitement awoke them to a state of fitful ferocity. *Much like the orcs*, Grace observed.

19

Moira looked down at the fletched arrow protruding from Ron's shoulder as he laid on his back, wheezing and pale, looking at her with surprise.

She reached and took the arrow with one hand, whilst she cut a notch into it either side and snapped it off, keeping the emotions from her face.

'Keep breathing, Ron, you'll not get away that easy,' she said.

Her hands trembled as she turned to Zephyrus and told him to help her move Ron.

Zephyrus rushed over, almost fell to his knees as he reached to lift Ron from the ground. Moira reached out.

'Careful with him,' she said.

Zephyrus gave a hurried nod as he slowed himself down and slipped his hands under Ron's back.

He lifted Ron with ease and looked to Moira for direction. She gestured back the way they came, and he moved with as much care as circumstances allowed.

They moved into the trees and Zephyrus set Ron down on the ground. Moira reached into her pouch and chewed a pastille of herbs as she gestured for Zephyrus to move Ron onto his side.

'I must push it through, Zephyrus, keep the wound channel as small as we can, ok?' she said.

He nodded and took a deep breath as she passed him the knife.

'Cut two incisions in a cross so we can push the head through,' she said.

Zephyrus wrestled Ron's coat off his shoulders and then tore the tunic with his claws, revealing the swollen, bruised purple mark on his back. Zephyrus cut into his back in a cross pattern and looked up at Moira. She leaned from the waist and pushed the arrow through Ron's shoulder.

Ron stayed unconscious as Moira spat the chewed pastille onto the wound and massaged it before she tore a length of material from her sleeve and put it over the wound.

Zephyrus gagged at the sight of so much blood but kept Ron on his side.

'What now?' he said.

Moira looked at Ron with an anxious tenderness.

'Let him rest, if we can, but I can help it along,' she said.

Zephyrus smiled at her.

'You've some experience,' he said.

Moira blinked back tears and smiled at him. His heart thumped a little faster, impressed by her beauty in these circumstances.

'Shut up and let me chant, keep watch if you can, they'll smell the blood,' she said.

Zephyrus nodded as he stood up, looking at Ron, laying on the ground, bleeding and unconscious.

He clenched his fists and looked down the pass. There was movement in the shadows, too cautious to be orcs at play, and he asked Moira to give him her knife.

She looked up, about to ask why when she saw his expression and sighed.

'We'll fight them off, if we can,' she said.

Zephyrus frowned as he took the knife.

'I must be able to remember something,' he said.

Moira looked up from Ron.

'Stick them with the pointy end,' she said.

Zephyrus stared at the horizon, then weighed the dagger in his hand and took a deep, steadying breath.

'Good enough,' he said.

20

Zephyrus left Moira and Ron.

It's me they want, he thought, *and I led them through this place so I might gain some power back.*

The dagger was not the finest, a wooden hilt wrapped with leather and an iron blade hammered into sharpness. It looked small, fragile in his clawed hand but as he gripped it, a surge of wild courage rushed through him.

The arrow whistled past him, and he cried out as two men and a woman came forwards.

The woman held a longbow upright, arrow nocked as she grinned at him. Her skin was a deep tan, streaked with crimson war paint and hair braided into thin snakes tied away from her face. She wore a stained tunic and a long deerskin skirt slashed at the sides. She grinned at the sight of Zephyrus.

The two men behind her held swords in their hands. One was a redhead with a thick tangled beard festooned with small bones which rattled as he moved, His head shaved and he wore a faded leather vest, showing off scars, tattoos and a body honed from experience into a pallid weapon.

The other had hair longer than the woman's, unwashed and shining with grease as it fell about his face. He had a pointed face and piercing blue eyes which stared at a fixed point. Like his fellow warriors, he held a smile of anticipation which made Zephyrus' stomach churn.

Not anticipation, Zephyrus gauged, but zeal.

He thought of Ron and Moira and dropped the blade, putting his hands up as he mustered the largest smile he could.

'No more, please, no more,' he said.

They stopped and looked at one another. The woman lowered the bow as she appraised Zephyrus with care.

She barked out something crude to the men which made them laugh. One of them took out a length of rope from over his shoulder as he sheathed his sword. The long-haired man pointed his sword at Zephyrus and raised his chin.

'You will come with us, and no harm will come to you,' he said.

Zephyrus put out his hands, wrists pressed together as he lowered his head.

'I tire of running, even though it may mean my death,' he said.

The red bearded man came and tied Zephyrus' hands at the wrists. Without warning, he threw a tight punch into Zephyrus' abdomen, making him fold over at the waist as a further loop of rope went around his neck.

Zephyrus gasped as the ropes tightened. The lack of breath and the blow took him to his knees. The woman had returned her bow over her back. She picked up the knife and looked at it, sneering before she tossed it to the ground in front of him.

'Your surrender speaks volumes, abomination, but Lord Mercer wants you unharmed,' she said.

Zephyrus pushed his fears and thoughts of Ron and Moira from his mind. They had done enough, he decided, and they were never going to reach the Ethereal College. He would die without knowing the lightning again, and in pain, but it would be his death not anyone else's.

'See that I am, then,' Zephyrus said.

His words were staccato, spat against the tight band of rope pressing into his windpipe.

The woman sneered and helped Zephyrus to his feet. The four of them walked out of the Marrow Pass, and Zephyrus looked back, hoping they would understand, and in time, forgive his surrender.

He knew that he would soon be far from their reach, whether it be scorn or friendship. Zephyrus wished them well, in his heart.

21

Moira looked over her shoulder. The silence was a brooding, twitching beast at her back. She was unsure whether to wait, flee or treat Ron. The latter was urgent, but her sense of self-preservation made her eager to evade death, if only for a moment longer.

Ron was breathing, but still unconscious. The herbs were doing their work, and the bleeding had stopped.

Now, it was a matter of time and will.

No one came for them, and she sat with Ron, willing his eyes to open. The wound itself was not significant, but with the exhaustion and constant alertness, it became a source of concern. Ron, she knew, was strong, but strength itself was fleeting and it left the greatest of men when they needed it the most.

She studied his face and stroked the hair from his face as her heart shifted in her chest, like it was trying to escape her ribcage.

Moira kissed him on the forehead, eyes shut as tears fell from the corners.

'Please, Ron, come back to me,' she said.

He took in a deep, slow breath and groaned as his eyes opened.

'Couldn't stay away from you, Moira,' he said.

She sat up, smiling as she wiped her eyes.

'Zephyrus has gone, he said he went to observe, but I...' she said.

Ron swallowed, face tight with pain as he tried to sit up.

'He's gone? Surely he's not tried to reach the college?' he said.

Moira sighed and shook her head.

'No, I think he's either gone to fight them or to save us,' she said.

He stared up at the sky, fighting the serpentine sense of failure which snaked through his body.

'That's not his choice to make, Moira,' he said.

Moira lowered her head.

'It's the only choice left to him,' she said.

Ron grunted and sat up, one hand pressed against his shoulder. He shook his head, eyes turned to slits as he fought to control his demeanour. He asked Moira to help him up, and she did so, with care.

'Where are we going?' she said.

Ron leaned into her as another wave of dizziness washed over him.

'To fulfil my contract,' he said.

22

They dragged Zephyrus when his legs failed him, the two men bullying and kicking him whilst the woman took the lead, making them stop whenever she sensed a presence.

Zephyrus learned a great deal of vulgarities relating to his name, station, race and prowess, which he stored for later anecdotes.

If they allowed him such time to enjoy them, he thought.

They stopped after a few hours once they were clear of the Marrow Pass. Failure bit into him like a venomous snake, deadening his limbs and making his thoughts dry and brittle inside his skull.

'Why am I not dead?' he said.

The trio chuckled.

'You're worth more alive to Mercer,' the woman said.

Zephyrus shook his head as much as his bonds allowed.

'He sought me dead, abomination were his words, why don't you just kill me now?' he said,

The woman's hand came out, striking him across his face, hard enough to make his eyes water.

He sagged in his bonds, the moment's courage fleeing before the reality of his situation.

'I would, but we would take our time, half-dragon, do you want that?' the long-haired man said.

Zephyrus shook his head as the red bearded man heaved him to his feet.

'Enough of your questions, it's frustrating enough we don't get to hurt you, let alone drag your sorry arse all the way to Holme,' he said.

The woman looked up and Zephyrus saw her eyes roll back in her head as a thin trickle of blood splashed down her upper lip. She shuddered and staggered backwards. The other men said and did nothing, although the long-haired man looked at her with something approaching envy. The possession of a God left physical marks, and not all of them were celebrated.

She wiped her upper lip and grinned at them all.

'We don't have to drag his sorry arse all the way,' she said.

The two men laughed and pushed Zephyrus between them, letting him trip over his feet as the harsh rope scoured the skin over his throat. A fierce humiliation bloomed in his chest as they cut his breath off, and for a moment, the shape of a Phrase came to him.

'Mercer's coming to meet him, by divine appointment,' she said.

They looked at Zephyrus, and the long-haired man gave him a smile which made him shudder.

It frightened Zephyrus, because the expression was one uncharacteristic for such a man.

Pity.

23

They sat Mercer with his men, such as those remaining to him, when he felt a slow, uneven pressure building in his sinuses. He saw the blood splash down the front of his brocaded tunic as his men ignored it.

'WE HAVE HIM.'

It was the wet snap of breaking bone, the song of violation and revelation and the gelid burp of something which fed on feeling and lightness. The voice came in from everywhere, within and without.

'How. far?' he said.

His voice was a strained whisper, distant against the bolus of thoughts and sensations in his head.

'THE MARROW PASS.'

Despite the violation, Mercer smiled. A fluttering hope took wing within his chest as he opened his eyes. Soiled with blood, and slurring his wounds, Lord Mercer told his men to arrange for an escort.

He planned to collect his reward, and with it, his ascension.

24

Ron went to stand up, wobbling as he gritted his teeth, one hand pressed against the wound in his shoulder, but Moira caught him when his balance failed him.

'I know, I know, but your body has limits, Ron,' she said.

He grimaced as he eased himself onto the ground.

'It's been a while,' he said.

Moira smiled, despite herself.

'Since you fell into my arms?' she said.

Ron chuckled before the wound interrupted his reveries with a tight burst of pain, making him gasp.

'If I knew taking an arrow got me into your arms, I'd have been less careful,' he said.

Moira sighed and touched his cheek with the tips of her fingers. Her lips parted as they stared into one another's eyes. A light passed between them, a flush of heat rising to their skins as they shared a knowing, poignant look.

Moira kissed him on the cheek, but he turned his head and as his lips found hers, she gave a soft moan of delighted surprise at the first contact. Ron's hand came up to cup the back of her head, resting without imposing.

Ron tasted herbs on Moira's lips, the same ones which were helping his wound heal, a floral, astringent aftertaste which took him back to simpler times. Moira tasted copper and determination on his, and the faint tang of the leaf he smoked.

A moment, eternal and fleeting, passed between them. Ron drew back, his eyes unfocused as a lazy smile played on his features.

'Oh Ronnie,' she said.

Moira blinked back tears as she helped him to his feet.

'They can't have gotten far,' she said.

Ron looked past her, over the valley.

'The orcs will want their fun first,' he said.

She shook her head.

'It wasn't orcs, I'm sure,' she said.

Ron lowered his chin to his chest.

'Mercer's men?' he said.

Moira shook her head. Ron frowned, confused.

He held himself apart, feeling the prickling sense of failure pluck at his self-esteem.

'It doesn't matter, they'll have left a trail,' he said.

Ron took a deep breath as he brushed himself down. He looked at Moira, who nodded her agreement.

They made their way with intention, and when Moira found her dagger, abandoned in the grass, she held it up so Ron could see.

'I made you that,' he said.

Moira smiled as she slipped it back into the sleeve of her robes.

'The blade's still sharp,' she said.

Ron curled his upper lip, a mock arrogance lightening his features.

'Well,' he said.

Ron raised his hand for them to stop, as they heard movement. The guttural grunts of orc, which faded as they passed. Ron lowered his hand, and they moved again. It focused his attention on the ground.

Four individuals.

One of them had stumbled, dragged, judging by the trenches gouged into the powdered stone then hoisted upright.

Two men, judging by the footprints, one heavier than the other. Ron stopped and examined them. He nodded to himself, satisfied as he looked at the third set.

Smaller than the others, human but lacking the mass. An indentation in the powder prompted a curious finger then a pinch of the soil between his fingers.

Female. Archer, gauging by the pressure on each step. He could not be sure, but at the monastery, they taught principles which had worked throughout time.

The process eased some frustration and impotence he felt. Not all of it, and its analgesic properties were quite overrated, but it allowed Ron a sense that somehow he had a slight chance to retrieve his principal.

He looked at Moira, who watched him with a nervous curiosity.

'They've not gone far, we might catch them before they leave the pass,' he said.

She smiled with relief.

'I can't believe it of him, he has given himself up like that,' she said.

Ron looked down at where the dragged prints were then back up at Moira again.

'I can, but it is not us he needs to convince of his worth and courage,' he said.

Moira raised an eyebrow.

'Himself?' she said.

Ron winked at her.

'Yes, and that's what gets a principal killed, in my experience,' he said.

She tilted her head to one side.

'Why did he lie about needing the book?' she said.

Ron shut his eyes, going back through the conversations they had. The pain made it difficult to focus, but he recalled some expressions and evasions which made sense to him now.

'All men fear impotence. Even more so, if they fear themselves apart,' he said.

Moira frowned as she considered his words.

'He's a half dragon, borne from a divine egg, not much more apart than that,' she said.

Ron scratched his chin, bit back the spasm of pain as he moved his shoulder.

'Halfling is somewhere on the list,' he said.

She chuckled, as quiet as she could manage.

'You're unique,' she said.

He gave a graceful bow, digging into the marrow of himself to mask the discomfort.

'Anyway, enough navel gazing, let's go find my principal,' he said.

She exhaled and gave a pained smile.

'Good thing I came back, eh?' she said.

Ron's fingers went to his lips, tingling from the sense memory of their kiss. He spoke but thought better of it.

'Always, Moira, always,' he said.

25

They moved, emboldened by the most fragile of hopes, further into the Marrow Pass.

The cultists found patience difficult with the metallic scent of blood in their nostrils. Grace, being the closest in terms of faith and connection, saw the roiling frustration in Skett-Al and Edric, expressed in a constant drive to provoke Zephyrus. They were waiting in a grove, a mile beyond the pass. Mercer was coming to collect his prize in person.

Which interested her.

'What are you, besides a monster?' she said.

Zephyrus sniffed back the blood into his nose.

'I would ask you the same question, at least mine is by appearance rather than deed,' he said.

Grace grinned and squatted before him.

'Whatever thou wilt shall be the whole of the law,' she said.

Zephyrus sneered and spat a gobbet of pink saliva onto the ground between his feet.

'Spare me your borrowed sentiments,' he said.

She went to slap him but decided against it. The others had taken their fun, and Grace knew this was a provocation. Her degradations were more acute because it restrained them to subtle actions. She was not the brute here, and the relative detachment allowed her to see this half-dragon's words for what they were.

'So, in the contest between my borrowed sentiments, and your bold protestations, who do you believe to be the victor?' she said.

A light, blue and cold, flared in his eyes and for the first time, Grace felt a tickling apprehension as arcs of lightning danced between his teeth.

'My destiny is not complete,' he said.

Grace turned away, gestured to the others.

'Have your fun, don't kill him,' she said.

She did not look back, instead she enjoyed the subtle cruel delight in hearing the bravado beaten from the half-dragon.

Grace prayed that whatever Mercer had planned for it, she asked for one boon.

That it would hurt.

26

Moira realised as they walked, that they had not left the Marrow Pass.

'Ron, where are we going?' she said.

He rolled his head to ease the tension.

'We need the book, if we're to help him,' he said.

Moira tasted bitter panic at the back of her throat.

'I thought we were going to rescue him?' she said.

Ron raised an eyebrow.

'Oh we are, just with an extra step,' he said.

Moira struggled to control her distress.

'Wandering further into murder orc territory?' she said.

Ron put his hands up, and the wound in his shoulder pulled again, cutting the humour off at the neck.

'If Zephyrus is powerless, he's doomed,' he said.

Moira gestured past him.

'Someone's got him, doomed is a day late and a coin short,' she said.

Ron came towards her, put his hands out.

'We're quieter than he is, we go in, get the book and get out,' he said.

Moira sighed, her eyes bright with fear, as she glanced around her.

'If Mercer has him, it's a fool's errand,' she said.

Ron's eyes lowered as he took in a deep breath.

'If we're meeting a noble, it's rude to arrive without a gift,' he said.

Moira smirked at his presumption.

'Ron, you're wasting time, better to find him first isn't it?' she said.

Ron looked past her, his eyes unfocused for a second. He seldom allowed himself the luxury of despair, but sometimes he saw it in the drift of clouds or the soft caress of the wind. It passed, much like the weather.

'This is finding him,' he said.

Moira sighed and reached into the pouches on her belt, took out a pair of pastilles and put them in Ron's hand.

'Take these, they'll keep you moving and we shall see who's right, won't we?' she said.

Ron wanted to kiss her again, but Moira's terse expression gave him pause. His heart ached more than his shoulder but much like despair, pain was as much a luxury in his world.

He popped the pastilles into his mouth and chewed them. The sharp taste made his eyes water, but as the juices ran down his throat, a wave of excited analgesia washed over him, soothing and charging him with energy.

'You should sell these,' he said.

The green film on his teeth abated the impact of his charms. Moira, herself fighting the urge to kiss him again, smiled and shook her head.

'Perhaps we could make a business of it?' she said.

Ron raised an eyebrow.

'Stop body guarding?' he said.

Moira's lips parted, and her chest rose as she took a deep breath.

'We risk too much, too often, and as noble as it is, there are other paths we could take, Ron,' she said.

Ron swallowed and ran his tongue over his teeth underneath his lips. He stepped forwards, charged with purpose and placed his hand on her cheek. She lowered her face to his, and their lips pressed together. It was little more than a brush of their lips, but as they closed their eyes, they shared a fragile hope between them.

When they parted, Ron looked into her eyes and his gaze was as pure and certain as the dawn.

'Other paths sound good,' he said.

She drew back, testing the purity of his gaze and smiled at him. She reached out, brushed a green strand from the corner of his mouth.

'You need a shave,' she said.

He smiled and rubbed his chin with the tips of his fingers.

'A bath too, I imagine,' he said.

A weighted silence hung between them. Ron stirred at the image of Moira sat across from him, in an ocean of suds and steaming water, and he saw in her eyes much the same thought. They put it in the box of unspoken things, however as Ron took a small step backwards.

Ron and Moira continued through the Marrow Pass.

Experience and familiarity had them moving with care, and they made their way through the winding paths to the Ethereal College.

Moira felt it before they saw it. A tenderness in her abdomen, the slow waxing of a cramp in her calves. Whispers of knowledge which curled around her perceptions. The tragedy of a ruined library was abstract to her, compared to the purity of nature but she felt the loss, and the wound it had left in the world.

The remains of the college were visible, set atop a plateau about thirty feet above them, the shards of black glass gleaming in the afternoon sun. A place felt as much as seen, Moira thought, as Ron stood with her.

'They didn't leave much,' he said.

Moira took his hand in hers.

'We'll find it, if it's there,' she said.

Still holding hands, they made their way up the hill as Moira fought the whispers which gained volume with every step.

27

In his carriage, Mercer sat and focused on the future.

Whenever he turned his perceptions inwards, away from the trappings of power, all he saw were scars and missing places. Within those missing places, he knew, were the true signs of power.

He had always been ambitious, a familial trait which took his bloodline from peasants to nobility within a few generations.

Merchants by trade, and ostracised for their use of usury, the Mercers parlayed their status through the careful use of loans to militia in the earliest days of the Vivarian Empire. Ansel looked back at the men and women of his line and wondered what they would have thought about his left-handed rise to power.

She had come to the castle, much as Zephyrus did.

Not, however, as obvious a person of power as Zephyrus, and it was this difference which made her seduction and recruitment of Mercer far easier to complete.

Mercer would lie with her, trace the runic scars on her bare flesh as they laid together, wondering how they ever lived without one another. The facts of his seduction evaded his sight, and as he gained power and influence in his faith, it stole pieces of the man he had been.

Keeley.

Her name had been Keeley.

Within these empty places, he knew how his recruitment had hastened her own advancement, before his. They passed, and he continued to live as though all the decisions made were his own.

He returned to the present as a splash of blood fell down his upper lip. Dabbing it away with a swipe of his fingers, he studied his fingers with a removed perspective.

Podswark sat across from him, a neutral expression on his face. Podswark was recalling the faces of the family of the squire who they had buried the day before. Lord Mercer had not attended the service, and judging by his manner, would not have recalled his attendance, anyway.

'We'll be there, soon,' Podswark said.

Podswark handed him a handkerchief and Mercer took it without acknowledgement, wiped his face and passed it back.

Mercer thanked him. He kept on touching the empty places in his head, wondering what would come back to him when he had the half-dragon's heart in his hands, offered to his God.

28

Read these words. Whose voice do you hear them in?

Language has power. Captured in fragile forms, altering the shape of the brain and consciousness within it.

To learn these structures, in their more advanced forms was an invitation.

Sometimes, Moira thought, an unwelcome one.

The cool, green articulation of her Midwifery still reached out to some darker places.

Such as whatever remained within the Ethereal College. Old words carved into the earth, running through the veins of plants. Carried on the wind. She had an ear for it, unlike Ron, who dealt with what he could hit and see.

Yet she knew it would help them find the book.

Paper was a fine place for life. Time introduced the smallest things to rest upon its surfaces. Midwifery taught Moira to observe at the smallest level. What lived there, sometimes was not kind to being observed.

Things which could observe her.

'Ron?' she said.

He looked at her over his shoulder. Raised an eyebrow.

Moira looked at the earnest light in his eyes.

'These sorts of places, they're not good for a midwife,' she said.

He turned around.

'I have to find this for him. You get yourself away, if they've got him, then you're safe,' he said.

She clasped her fingers and pressed her palms together, rested them against her stomach, which ached with fear and a sense of reproach.

'I'm not saying I am going. I just have to be careful here, these kinds of places, they speak to our kind,' she said.

He nodded.

'I've guarded all kinds. Language is power,' he said.

She smiled and came towards him. Taking his hand, she squeezed his fingers, enjoyed the rough strength and calluses as he squeezed back.

'Let's not dwell here,' she said.

He took her hand, pressed it to his lips and closed his eyes.

'You're my principal,' he said.

Her eyes prickled but an instinct not to feed anything here too much of herself lent her a sense of control which made her stand back.

'Then take care of me, Ron Brandywood,' he said.

He led her up the hill. The air grew damp and cold as they drew closer.

Orcs had their fun.

It was difficult for them to build anything, easier to destroy. However, the tragedy had been how the institution destroyed itself.

Moira's sinuses pinched as they wandered past the jagged remains of a black glass pillar, crusted with dried blood which ran down its sides in thick rivulets of black glue.

Ron stopped, stared at the gallery of remains, rubble in piles, the bleached remains of window frames, and everywhere, the bloated corpses of books. Some of them, Moira knew, would have contained useful knowledge or observations about the world which might have saved a life, or destroyed one.

Death was part of life and within it laid a disdain for the wanton savage.

Moira understood the vagaries of all living things, yet here brutality, vandalism and ignorance had primed the ghosts of failed rituals and successful sacrifices to a new life.

Fingers caressed the back of her neck. She flinched, gave a small shout and knew she was in danger the longer she stayed here.

Ron reached for her.

'Run,' he said.

She gave a hurried nod, turned on her heels and ran.

A qliphothic thought, larger than life or death, unfolded itself inside her head. It allowed her a few steps before it took her over.

It began as a trembling in her calves, then thinned out into a series of stabbing sensations which ran up the backs of her thighs, and into the small of her back, plunging through into the meat of her hips and thighs before it burrowed into the pit of her stomach and grew fat on the seat of feelings which grew there.

The Midwives understood smaller lives existed within the flesh of all living things. Thoughts, too, much like this one.

It burst within her, used her weaknesses as fuel, and reached into them, recreated itself into vorpal splinters of resentment and fear.

A symphony of alien arrogance arranged against a chord progression of fear and self-loathing. It had once expressed love, phrased between two students who had found accommodation with one another. One celebrated, the other tested, and for a while it had flowed without incident beyond joy. Then, the tests overwhelmed the celebration and what was once sweet became bizarre and emasculating, then horrific.

Love made it a hearth god of rapacious hunger, and it fed on Moira.

Her last thoughts were of Ron's hand in hers, the press of his lips. The honeyed song of his voice, best expressed when in his cups, and at play slipped into the seething mass of the atonal phrase's gullet. Oblivion.

Her body, however, turned, and its lips drew back over her teeth as it took the dagger from its sleeve, then reached into the pouches on her belt, sprinkled something red onto the blade and then slid the edge down the middle of its bottom lip.

It flicked the blood away, and black smoke hissed from the blade. It crouched, held the blade forwards, turned the handle in her fingers with a smooth ripple, like a musician tuning an instrument.

Then it moved towards the halfling, eager to test the instruction given to it by the observations of the orcs who had fouled its tomb.

It laughed at the look of despair in his eyes as he stepped backwards, bringing his elbows into his sides and turning his feet inwards. His hands closed into fists, flowers blooming in reverse, buds dark and rough with application.

Ron retreated to a place of discipline within himself.

It was not Moira, he told himself, but something which has borrowed her.

29

The dagger flashed forwards, faster than anything Ron had seen in a long time, stabbing forwards to gauge the distance, the mark of a practiced knife fighter before it sent out a low kick, aiming for the meat of his thigh or the bundle of nerves behind his knee cap.

Ron darted backwards, leaning away as he watched it move, horrified into silence by the blank malevolence which twisted her face into a horrific parody. Her hair flew about her face and whatever warmth had existed there, fled from his sight as she slashed and kicked at him again.

A sour, oily scent exuded from her pores, at odds with the warm, plant-like smell he had known all the years of their acquaintance.

Ron caught himself, referring to her in the past sense, and his opponent punished the thought as the tip of the blade sliced into the meat of his left eyebrow.

It had been aiming for his eye, but the resulting wound poured blood into his field of vision, cloaking it in a thin film of scarlet before he dashed backwards, his feet moving underneath him, smooth against the ground. His hands were still by his sides, not reluctant but patient as he fought the most important battle.

Within himself.

It licked the blade, and Ron recalled the trail of smoke which came off it, as a crawling disorientation moved underneath his skin, creating spots of numbness throughout his face and growing as it moved down to the soles of his feet.

He blinked, swept away more blood from his wounded eyebrow as his legs buckled. The wound in his shoulder throbbed, eager to join the spreading weakness as his arm went numb all the way to his elbow.

Ron forced himself upright, focusing on his breathing as he twisted and ducked beneath its blows, the mark of a credible opponent as it lashed out at him, limbs in concert meaning he faced her kicks and the knife.

Whatever coated the blade insinuated itself into his blood, but Ron allowed his world to refine into nothing more than breath and motion. There was a place which did not recognise the face of his opponent, and without the armour of that intimacy, he knew he could accept the reality of their situation.

He was going to die at the hands of his love, if he did not.

Ron's vision blurred as a further wave of disorientation shook him and he went down onto one knee, turning the blade away as he struck out with his right hand, allowing the knife to follow its natural arc as he turned to one side, allowing the kick to hit air when his hip had been.

The impact of his blow against her wrist reverberated through the bones of his knuckles, travelling down as his forearm as the bones broke with a nauseous crack. When he looked, her expression had not

changed, the injury not affecting her
determination to kill him.

She changed the dagger to its other hand
without missing a beat. Ron gauged the
relentless pace of her attack and wagered
the poison would soon overwhelm him
enough to fall prey to it.

Ron looked into her eyes, hoping for a sign
Moira was still in there. When their eyes
met, Ron gazed into a dark absence which
wore her face like a mask, an armour forged
from affection and sentiment, now abused
and reworked into a weapon designed to
murder him for the reticence he had to hurt
someone he loved.

He had loved her for so long, and with such
reserve, that it hurt more than the poison did
to see it gone from her face. The pain, and
the anger which masked it, lent power to his
limbs even as the spots of numbness
spread through his body.

When she struck again, he let the knife
come forwards, as his fingers circled her
wrist and with tears in his eyes, he pulled
her arm towards him, letting the blade
plunge into the wound she had treated a

few hours before as he bought his forearm across his body and slammed it upwards into her elbow joint.

The snap was loud and when Moira screamed, Ron's head throbbed with anguish more potent than any of the poison running through his veins. He felt something thick and warm splash down his chin and onto his chest. Its sour ordure meant it was not blood, but vomit and yet it did not stop him from continuing to press his advantage.

A final race against the poison and grief, as he let the broken arm flail away and caught her ankle in the palm of his hand and slid it up to cup her toes.

Tears ran down his face, remembering a solitary foot massage after a hard day's ride fleeing Aldmera, and the appreciative whimpers, the unspoken intimacies which had fed something between them.

Ron wrenched her foot and shoved her backwards. She toppled onto the ground, shrieking in words which made him want to weep and vomit until he was hollow. He looked at her, the perspiring and crippled shell of his friend and perhaps, in time, lover, and a spasm of debilitating anguish erupted from the pit of his stomach.

Grief. Poison. Injury.

All the same thing to him as he stood there.

'Let her go,' he said.

His voice was a harsh, metallic bark.

'Give her back to me, you've made your point,' he said.

She cackled, the bleak light of madness animating her features as she revelled in his suffering.

'Never,' it said.

Ron fought another wave of nausea, staggered back to give himself some room. His vision blurred and his breath grew hot and thick in his lungs. He focused on his breath, went into the parts of his mind honed into perfect libraries of discipline and movement.

It was faster, without the care or control for self-preservation which guided an opponent in control of themselves.

To guard against that, he required a similar lack of self-preservation.

Ron turned his left side towards her, bobbed on the balls of his feet and tucked his elbows into his sides, hands up to guard his face. Well, his throat, groin and under his armpits, which would kill him if she took the knife there. The equation of taking damage did not include the time he had left.

He would go down fighting, he promised himself. Then, he would find Moira again, or he would walk away from this moment.

It moved forwards, slashing the blade in a diagonal arc of descent, turning the dagger over in her hand as her ruined arm flailed and she balanced on one foot. Ron tucked himself close to her, grabbed the front of her robe and hopped forwards, driving his knee into the side of her supporting leg.

The momentum moved the knee with a sickening crack, as Ron swung his elbows up underneath her chin in a pair of rapid slices. Her head snapped back, and gravity took her down. She swiped with the dagger, cutting a lock of Ron's hair from his head as he followed her down, climbing up to wrap his legs around her chest.

He jabbed at the inside of her elbow with his index finger, and her fingers stiffened, letting the dagger fall from her grasp as she wailed, offended by the failure of her borrowed flesh as they fell together.

Ron took his face in her hands. He willed for a sign she was still there, some small spark amidst the darkness which was his world right now.

Nothing, and with that, he looked into her eyes, told her he loved her and then wrenched her head to the right with a grisly snap. The life shuddered out of her, and yet he held her face in his hands, weeping until a last wave of weakness offered him a chance to leave this moment, and at his lowest ebb, he accepted. Ron collapsed forwards onto Moira, as he passed out.

30

Zephyrus shifted in his bonds, putting a tongue against a fang knocked loose in its socket when he asked for water. They were not stopping at night, keen to deliver their prize to Mercer and this pace meant these men were the kind to find difficulty in routine and endurance. It made them children, and so they took it out on him.

Alive didn't mean it excused him from pain.

The jab at his face.

Open handed slaps.

Sharp, accurate kicks to his hip or thigh. The pooling blood which burned with each step, limping in a seesawing gait which made his lower back throb.

Punches to one of his livers, jabs to his windpipe to 'make sure he didn't use any phrasing'.

He wept in silence, but as his tears burned and irritated, so did his decision to allow this to overwhelm him.

It was tedious. Tedium offended him - it was an affront to his destiny.

From tedium came resentment, and despite the gallery of injuries, they grew less effective in humiliating him.

A soul-numbness crept over him with every indignity he received.

They had stopped within the borders of Alsace, lands assigned to Ignus, but held for the commons, so they would be undisturbed. Zephyrus heard them say Mercer was coming in person, but he had not seen a messenger bird, or a blind drop accessed. The two men were idiots, so he spoke to the woman, who kept her own counsel. She looked at him with a polite indifference.

'How are you speaking to Lord Mercer?' he said.

She frowned and adjusted her gauntlets before she looked up.

'None of your concern, half-dragon, and I will not tell you,' she said.

Zephyrus snorted in derision which made her raise an eyebrow.

'Remind me who's bound here?' she said.

Zephyrus fought the thin hum of alarm at the change in tone, but then realised his remark had hit a nerve. His social ineptitudes here had served him well.

'I have a certainty you will never know,' he said.

He cringed inward, but the florid phrase denoted a confidence which further unnerved the woman.

The resulting cuff across the back of his head was a validation, not a punishment.

The ugly buzzing in his left eardrum was a victory march, and although he needed a minute to settle his vision, he threw caution to the wind and enjoyed being himself for a change.

'Grubby, malnourished malcontents such as you will not cow nor curtail my destiny,' he said.

Grace smiled. Zephyrus shuddered at the cold, dark light which appeared in her eyes. She lifted her chin.

'YOUR DESTINY IS AS ALL LIVING THINGS, TO DIE UNMOURNED AND INSIGNIFICANT.

'MEAT TO FUEL THE PLEASURES OF MY
RAPACIOUS PURSUIT OF ECSTASY,
BUT OTHERWISE YOUR POWER ONLY
SERVES BY ITS ENDING.

'DO

'YOU

'UNDERSTAND?'

The voice did not come from any human
throat. It appeared within him, an uninvited
guest who helped themselves to the
contents of your larder or library. Divine
origin or not, there were gods he feared.

These were two of them.

'I thought they confined your worship to a
few sad orgies and a spot of light stabbing
disguised as ritual sacrifice?' he said.

Grace jerked to her feet, then lifted into the
air so her toes grazed the grass and she
stared at Zephyrus with a baleful hatred
which ruined all the humanity within her. A
slave, he decided, and the truth had cost
him, but it had felt good to speak from within
his considered assessment of a situation. It
had given him solace, but here it had armed

him, even as he looked into the raging eyes of twin Gods.

'YOU KNOW NOTHING OF POWER, EXCEPT TO SERVE IT.'

Zephyrus wiped betraying tears from his eyes, but he took in a deep breath and stared into her eyes.

'Yet here you are, scrabbling for sacrifices, sending common thugs to do your work, what sort of Gods are you?' he said.

'THE SUBTLE KIND.'

Zephyrus laughed and shook his head.

'Slit my throat now, it would be better than to serve something so...small,' he said.

The woman laughed, a grating, dry cackle which set his teeth on edge before she sat down and slumped forwards. She sat there for a moment before her breathing softened and she gave a strangled, disgusted cry as she lifted her head and wiped blood from her upper lip and chin. As she stared at Zephyrus, the firelight had turned the blood black, and she resembled some fierce savage in war paint, her lips pulled back over her teeth as she snarled at him.

She slapped him, but it was a kiss which tasted of triumph, not pain.

He spat the dislodged fang into the dirt and glared at the woman.

'There, see how much power you can beg for, from that,' he said.

The hand went up, and Zephyrus waited for it.

She turned away from him, returned her attention to the flames.

Edric came over and shoved him backwards, straddling him as he pressed the edge of a dagger to Zephyrus' cheek.

'Spit all the shit you want, you're still just meat, so be quiet,' he said.

Zephyrus smiled, despite the pain in his upper back and shoulders. The blade was an abstraction, and what fear sat in his bones, diluted by exposure.

'Correction, I am meat with value,' Zephyrus said.

Zephyrus, using his weakened stomach muscles, heaved himself first onto his side then upright.

Despite his bonds and injuries, Zephyrus sat, nursing a long-forgotten state of being within him, cradling its fragile flame from the cold winds of reality.

Hope.

31

He woke with the smell of blood in his nostrils, and the jagged thoughts left on the shore of himself, shining and sharp enough to cut if he stepped on them.

Each breath was a shallow, burdened pilgrim travelling from his lips to his lungs. An arduous journey on a staircase of bone and tissue. Some made it, others did not, but there were enough to prove the faith in continuing to exist.

Moira laid underneath him, cooling and broken. Ron reached a shuddering hand up and cupped her cheek, pressed his face into the meat of her shoulder and sobbed. He had enough air and will for that, at least, he thought.

The spasms wrenched him from within. He wept for what was, what might have been and what would be. Facts, hopes, dreams mourned for every fibre of his being. Yet despite his prayers and the depths of his grief, whatever Gods he knew, had turned their faces from his sight.

He rolled onto his side, stared up at the sky and took inventory.

His left arm was numb, a thin, persistent film of perspiration coated his skin and carried a cloying sweetness to his senses and his legs tingled with a warring series of sensations. Ron focused on his breath, the ritual separation which allowed a man some measure of control over his situation.

Not like this, he told himself.

The sky above was black, a few twinkling stars peering out between thick banks of cloud, like spies at a funeral. He focused on one star, calmed his breathing and felt a good breath reach the base of his lungs. Just one, but it was a build upon.

Now, for the next stage, he decided.

The first lesson in the monastery was how to fall. Some more assumptive and arrogant students had mocked this instruction, but Ron understood and the worth of it came back to him as discovered treasure.

Ron understood that falling caused an immediate lesson in how to get back up.

He tensed the muscles in his hips and thighs, clenched his abdominals and heaved himself upright. Right hand against the ground for purchase, and his left arm, dead against his side.

Sitting up felt worse, but it was something, Ron thought.

He didn't look at Moira. It would make him fall back and surrender, so he focused on the next stage.

All recoveries were kata or symphony, composed and suited to the instruments or practitioner. In a world where swords were more common than smiles, an empty hand needed more knowledge than most if it were to avoid death.

His breathing eased. Losing sensation abated, settling for whatever damage it had done whilst it had been fresh in his body, and so Ron, with a crippled, jerking clumsiness got to his feet and stood up.

'Now, where the hell is this book of yours, Zeph?' he said.

With no more concern than putting one foot in front of the other, Ron searched for the Lightning Thesaurus.

32

Fort Huntingdon had been a station for supplies during the last conflict, manned by a few, incompetent men and their disappointed families. A life, yes but one which existed underneath the vagaries and shadows cast by nobility. A place where good things happened if nothing did.

A carriage, driven by horse, rattling down the road towards them was an ill-omen for the men and women of Fort Huntingdon.

 The crest of House Mercer emblazoned on the side added cool depth to their concerns.

A stocky man with a solid round belly straining his tunic and wide shoulders came out. Down the path rode a brace of men and horses, and he addressed those whose curiosity had gotten the better of them. He looked over at them.

'Back to your duties, we shall not be here long,' he said.

Their duties, such as they were, became welcome respite from the vagaries of a noble. It was less work to turn your head to what was happening, and it relieved Podswark as he turned and told his lord the men were coming and they would prepare the thought.

'Did you bring the tithe?' Mercer said.

Podswark nodded, referring to the pouch on his belt. Stuffed with diamonds and given to the men who were bringing the half-dragon to them. Podswark was glad this was a truncated exchange, as these parts of his lord's life held a distinct unease for him.

A devout man in words, not deeds, Podswark kept the stories of his childhood. The slow, crawling corruption of The Rot, the twin decadence of The Chained Siblings were all prevalent in his thoughts as he watched his lord move through the stages of belief.

Whether this was an ascent or a descent, he could not say.

Lord Mercer, in the noble banns, was the son of adherents and spoke the same words but Podswark and most of those who served him knew this was polite fiction. They measured his true faith in calls to privacy, ignorance of bizarre actions and disposal.

Once, this had been a simple acknowledgement for Podswark, that men of power acted one way in private and another before their people. Such actions demanded, but this had grown to something which troubled even a simple man like him.

Mercer had a small holding, not much in the way of lands but it was fertile, good earth and untroubled by war, but Podswark saw the taint of corruption and how it was harming the peace they all enjoyed.

It had been small things, sour milk and accidents.

The bodies carried away, broken but sometimes still breathing.

The cries of horror, some of them from him.

Sometimes Mercer would have entire meetings with his men and not recall a single word said. Podswark arranged a scribe at all such affairs, unless it was something which no one wanted committed to the word.

More of those meetings, too.

He resented how he had become an apogee for his master. In the simple matters of state and rulership, Podswark held a blunt, pragmatic view of all actions they ordered him to take. Those at the bottom served those at the top, and the men in the middle, like him, worked to ascend or descend as their hearts demanded.

Podswark evoked a great deal of energy remaining in place.

Even as he wondered how long the House of Mercer would last. It was being defiled from within, and no one had the courage to say it aloud.

Not even him. A pox or an accident would have been a nobler ending, even without an heir beyond a crippled cousin entertaining pillow women in Hanju. Mercer had told him that once, when in his cups, and laughed.

Podswark paid deference to the station, but the man underneath was someone he had once liked, and now he vacillated between two ugly emotions.

Fear.

Pity.

They were states in which his own thoughts had taken root. Here they were, collecting a half-dragon who had killed his men, kept alive for some unknown purpose. Podswark guessed it was more complex than addressing an insult, but he had stayed in position by knowing when not to speak.

Or see.

Or listen.

The men arrived and Lord Mercer came out. He looked sallow and exhausted, wilting with the oppressive heat inside the carriage. His iced wine had melted to a pink soup in his goblet and some of it had stained his tunic, leaving a mark which looked like he had bitten his lip and spat down himself.

Podswark noted how it summed up his lord so well. He saw the men trying not to react.

'We'll take possession of him. Tie him tight where you can, muzzle him for fear of his Phrasing,' he said.

The men looked to one another then nodded their agreement.

Mercer told them to set up in the fort. He would be in his chambers and called only when the prisoner was there. He turned to Podswark and sighed.

'You can take care of the rest?' he said.

Podswark gave a slight nod and straightened his posture.

'Aye, my lord,' he said.

Mercer gave a pained smile and looked around him.

'See no one speaks of this,' he said.

Podswark swallowed, the small moment of pride gone, swallowed by a leviathan of duty taken to the point of madness.

Silence, to Mercer, paid in iron.

He looked at the men and women of Fort Huntingdon, only twelve. Peasants with blunted blades.

Podswark stared at the men and took a deep breath.

'You heard your Lord,' he said.

Some of them looked appalled, but they hid it well. The rasp of swords swung out in the air and some people, who had been watching, gasped as their fears gained hair and height.

They were professionals. It was quick and helped by the fact some of them did not fight. One or two looked at Mercer and Podswark with expressions of reverence as they knelt down and took a blade to the back of their head. Mercer watched and then went inside. Podswark watched him leave, his head ablaze with concerns made feral by circumstance.

33

Burying Moira had cost him two fingernails, a dislocated little finger and a layer of skin. He had used the dagger to loosen the hard earth then worked with his remaining hand, kneeling over and scrabbling like a mad dog. He crawled over and dragged Moira's body over to the grave.

He vowed he wouldn't leave her to the predators of Marrow Pass. She was in no position to answer him, no matter how he wished things were different.

Moving her in was a matter of leverage, then as she had fallen onto her front, moving her into position and looking at her face, still and slack with absence. He closed her eyes, then wiped the smears of blood and dirt he left with his palm.

Ron buried her with care, tears flowing and embracing the constant, building library of wounds he had collected.

Much like the one he still had to search.

He staggered to the remains, shelves collapsed in on themselves, swollen with books. Nature had not been kind to the collection, let alone the vandals who had availed themselves of the opportunity to destroy something beautiful.

Ron's hand was a blur, snatching and flipping open books, as his left still hung by his side, tingling but refusing to work with an adolescent petulance. He scanned the titles, where he could read them then set them to one side. He paid attention to everything, the texture and age of the paper, the condition of the ink. Even the shapes of the words, those in languages beyond his understanding were given consideration.

A small pile grew and the pace of the work had him remove his coat. The ache in his shoulder spiked then died out. It was not as bad as the pain in his fingers.

His world focused down to the words before him. Ron had worked with mages before and understood some theory behind it. Not enough to Phrase, but then he knew some signs which accompanied them. He tested the knowledge through his understanding, the desperate translation of works rendered incomplete or illegible by time, and against it, was the raw need to find the book.

It would mean Moira had died for something.

At his hand, an unkind thought observed.

He ignored it. In the space between reaching for a particular book and the dismissal of the thought, a moment arose and blessed everything with its kindness.

The book arced with blue electricity when he opened it.

'Oh thank you,' he said.

Ron closed it and wiped his eyes.

He checked to make sure. His understanding of dragon was rudimentary, but he recognised a few words by their shapes, and one word confirmed his suspicions.

Shochraos.

Lightning.

He tucked it under his arm, picked up his coat and limped away from the Ethereal College. Looking at the grave, he gave a soft, determined grunt and was on his way.

34

Zephyrus limped with his head down, not resisting the persistent tug of the rope and without looking up to react. It drained the enthusiasm from Edric and Skett-Al, and Grace had not looked at him since he had humiliated her and forced a possession.

Inside his head, Zephyrus searched for something.

A break in Phrasing came about for several reasons.

Saying the words was one part but Phrasing demanded a mental connection, discipline and repetition built atop a firm foundation of faith in its achievement.

Losing the lightning pained him. His anxiety grew confident and fat on the meat of his loss. Yet, here he existed in a place, beyond exhaustion, facing if not death then something ritual and unpleasant, and he realised none of it mattered.

There were other languages he knew. Not enough to Phrase aloud, but the theory was there. Now all he needed was a way to have them make sense aloud.

Desperation lent him faith.

They had not gagged him. The inherent flamboyance of his heritage had hidden the real dangers about him from their assessment. This pleased and frightened him. Either they did not know, or they did not care.

He was familiar with arrogance. It had led him here.

This realisation was like grit on the tongue of his mind. His thoughts gagged, flexed and changed as the blend of emotions attached themselves to the fragments of a Phrase in Social Influence.

He broke down the icon, recalled fragments from speaking lightning, finding common forms which would fit and expand upon the original meaning.

'vdri,' he said.

Edric, Skett-Al and Grace stopped. She had time enough to turn, reaching to pull the bow from where it sat across her back, when her eyelids fluttered and she fell forwards. In his peripheral vision, Edric and Skett-Al fell onto their sides.

The sound of gentle snores arose in the air.

Zephyrus hobbled away, but he stopped.

Closing his eyes, he vowed to do what was necessary.

He found a blade, cutting the ropes over a slow, shuddering process, hoping the blade would not slip and cut him. Then he stood up and glanced at the blade in his hand then down at the sleeping bodies.

One blow. Turning their faces away so he did not have to look at them. Driving the blade into the hollow of the throat and twisting. The sound alone flooded his mouth with bile, but he did each of them without malice or too much guilt.

Zephyrus looked around him, then turned and headed back to the Marrow Pass.

He missed having a bodyguard. *No*, he corrected himself, *he missed them*.

35

Ron kept his attention on his breath. The ground beneath his feet, the sky above, all became abstractions and consciousness itself surrendered to the simple animal rhythms of existence. The poison in Moira's blade did not impose further on him, but it had left its mark.

Poisons were not his area of expertise, but he knew some did not finish their work until death and despite his agonies, it had not killed him. A thin film of perspiration made his skin gleam, forced him to rake his damp hair away from his face and made his beard wet.

He endured.

The constant churn of his guts became a burden: carrying a shifting, larval heated mass in the pit of his stomach. He had not eaten since last night, so fasting became another way to purge himself of his condition.

Yet, the acts of breath and motion, drawing on what few resources he had left, were not alien to Ron. The poison in his veins from Moira's blade, but also the bitter draught poured into the hollow recesses of his heart.

Whatever had possessed her, was beyond his means to avenge. This left an acrid taste at the back of his throat, a mockery of the taste of her lips on his, and with it, every swallow became a sob.

Ron's breathing deepened as he kept moving. Sometimes, he staggered and once, stumbled over his feet, skinning his palms against the rough ground and hitting his wounded shoulder. He got up again, shook himself down and kept moving.

The black spots across his vision were like flowers, they had their seasons, blooming and dying with each step.

He stopped at a copse. Resting against the trunk, he closed his eyes for a second, and enjoyed the breeze against his skin.

Trying hurt, but it was all he had left.

He looked at the horizon, saw a single shape against it, darting forwards and trying to move without being seen. When the shape turned its head, he recognised the elongated maw and blinked to clear the spots from his eyes.

Ron shook his head. His laugh was high, broken and had a touch of madness swimming amidst the relief.

He pushed himself away from the tree, wiped his face, despite the sting of the cuts in his palms and moved to meet his principal.

The thumping of his heart was louder than anything.

As he drew closer, another thumping sound overrode the rhythms of his self.

Hooves.

He was close enough to see him. The fraternal look of confusion and relief.

36

Zephyrus did not understand why Ron was waving to his right and kept moving towards him.

Ron saw the plumes of dust being raised and was aghast Zephyrus had not.

Too late, Zephyrus had turned as the riders came over the hill. Four men, two having nocked arrows on bows and the others with swords drawn, pointing at him.

Ron watched as Zephyrus took an arrow to the chest before the horses were upon him. He ducked down, saw them swoop up his body and heave it onto the back of the horse. A few punches to soft areas to further enforce his compliance.

They rode away, and with it, Ron's bonhomie, fragile as it had been, followed.

He closed his eyes. Listening to the hooves, he gauged their speed and distance. These paths were not unknown to him, but they were unwelcome. A decision awaited him. Behind him, the grave of someone who had believed in him, and his work.

Ron kept his attention on his breath.

The ground beneath his feet, the sky above, all became abstractions and consciousness itself surrendered to the simple animal rhythms of existence.

He endured.

37

Mercer's faith, ragged by its corrosion, was steadfast and the divine relieved him of ambiguity, yet they did not come. They were supposed to arrive at dusk.

He watched the lengthening shadows as he drank iced wine and furrowed his forehead. Nostrils flaring with each breath as a shifting, clawed concern wrapped itself around the base of his skull.

'I'll send men,' Podswark said.

Mercer nodded without looking. He wanted to avoid the look in his man's eyes for it reflected his own feelings on the matter.

No one sought failure less than a nobleman.

Podswark walked away, and Mercer returned to the study of the shadows. Then, he raised his head and spoke.

'If the abomination lives, wound him if you have to, but he lives,' he said.

Podswark stopped and turned, gave a terse nod.

He walked on, hand on the hilt of his sword.

Mercer ignored the way Podswark's shoulders dropped as he walked away.

There were other men, loyal and less willing to entertain doubts, Mercer told himself.

Podswark had utility, and his own mind, two assets to any wise noble, but he had too much of the latter and no genuine talent to mask his feelings on certain situations.

Mercer smiled, and the broken places in his mind rubbed together.

The message came through, like lightning and a blade ran down his spine.

'IT HAS ESCAPED THEM. A PHRASE, THEN A KNIFE.'

Mercer grimaced as the goblet fell from his hand, splashing wine and ice onto the stone.

'This...is...unfortunate,' he said.

'THE ABOMINATION HAS FOUND POWER AGAIN.'

Mercer sagged in his seat.

'They've gone to find them,' he said.

'GOOD. IT SPOKE TO ME, I WILL ENJOY FEEDING UPON IT.'

Appetite, Mercer thought, *all they were was appetite*.

So was he.

Their power increased in line with it, and although he had gained from it, there had been a cost to him.

Demanded and paid repeatedly.

'It is my will to serve,' he said.

'IT IS.'

The voice rippled with a perverse satisfaction, and Mercer arched his back, like a cat. It was a reminder that, for all the pain, there was pleasure too. As he lost the taste of fresh bread, an unnoticed theft, Mercer got to his feet and went to update Podswark on the situation.

38

They rode back, uncaring for Zephyrus beyond ensuring they secured him at the wrists, ankles and across his mouth. One man, with a balding pate and tobacco-coloured eyes, took special care to ensure his immobility, but there was a pensive, almost pitying look in his eyes as he did so.

Zephyrus tried to speak. Sought for a Phrase which could transcend his bonds, but such things were beyond him. Pain erased the fragile sense of self-control he had regained and so, he surrendered for a time.

A brief journey across the plains.

Zephyrus saw the squat, dull fort and caught burned pork in his nostrils. It left a greasy aftertaste with each breath, and his stomach roiled with hunger.

Then he saw the pile of bodies and all appetite fled from him.

They stopped and pulled Zephyrus from the back of the horse. The balding man smiled at Zephyrus as he asked for a knife and cut the arrow in half then told one man to get a brand. Another man came towards them and held Zephyrus in place as they pushed the arrow through the meat of his shoulder.

His last thought before he passed out was a surprise at how gentle they were being with him. Then the pain overwhelmed him. The weight of hands beneath his armpits, the faint smell of his own flesh burning where they cauterized the wound. The splash of water on his face, and, the untying of his bonds before they lay him down on a bed. These things roused him from unconsciousness.

He opened his eyes, looked at the bald man and his sad smile. It was worse than the overt cruelty of Grace and her companions, because he had no defence against kindness.

'I'm sorry, for what it's worth,' he said.

Zephyrus nodded, his throat tight with emotion.

The man stood back.

'There's no sense fighting. Not anymore,' he said.

Zephyrus looked away, blinking back tears of frustration and weakness. Then he wiped them and stood up.

'No, you're right,' he said.

Zephyrus adjusted his robes, now stained and ragged beyond recognition and arched his back.

'Perhaps this is my destiny, and it is one which I will meet with courage and an open heart,' he said.

The man nodded and stepped to one side.

'He is waiting,' he said.

The smell of incense, rich and sharp, billowed into the room.

'BRING HIM TO US.'

The bald man looked on, detached from what was to come, but he looked at Zephyrus with pity as he stepped backwards and gestured for him to leave the room.

Zephyrus' legs shook with fear, but he took a deep breath and went to face his destiny.

Ron watched the fort, trusting to his senses, dulled by exhaustion as he gauged the situation.

One of his arms didn't work, his bowels were a riot, he was cut, bruised and grieving. There were at least four men he knew of, all armed and trained.

He gauged it as even.

To overcome one man with intent and purpose was to overcome a thousand.

Ron had to overcome himself. The challenge, and the conviction to face it was always the greatest test of his life, and one he faced every single day.

He stood up, stretched as much as his injuries allowed and took a deep breath. He thought of Moira and let the ache run through him as he walked towards the fort. He had tucked the book under his arm, but he took it and held it in his good hand, finding the solid weight of it reassuring.

Zephyrus looked at Ansel Mercer and fought the urge to comment. The dark circles under his eyes, the pallid complexion and the weight of oil in his hair, making it adhere to his scalp. His clothes were stained and worn, and the zeal in his eyes reminded him of Grace and the others.

'You never knew your worth, Zephyrus,' he said.

There was a tremor to his voice which betrayed either excitement or sickness, and Zephyrus wondered if Mercer could tell them apart.

Zealots sealed themselves to avoid seeing beyond their own boundaries. The sight and sound of Mercer made for an uncomfortable but accurate recognition, in so far as Zephyrus too, had known a similar hallucination of self appointment and self-image.

Destiny. Divinity. All the same if it led to the same place.

Madness.

Zephyrus looked at the ground.

'I did. It was why I ran,' he said.

Ansel raised an eyebrow in surprise at the deadpan tone.

'And you got further than I believed possible, well done,' he said.

Zephyrus looked about him then stared at Mercer.

'Not far or fast enough,' he said.

Mercer nodded.

'Still, credit to you, outside of your Phrasing, you possess qualities which surprised me,' he said.

Zephyrus gave a tight smile, unwilling to mention neither Ron nor Moira.

'Your gods, too,' he said.

Mercer frowned before his features twisted into a spasmodic mask and Zephyrus knew another conversation was coming.

'NO, WE SAW THE AID YOU WERE GIVEN.'

Their voice was the wet twist of violation. It made Zephyrus nauseous to feel it in his head.

'I traded it for a fleeting hope of power,' Zephryus said.

'POWER IS NOT FLEETING.'

Zephyrus did something once thought incongruous.

He laughed.

'I wager you wouldn't understand how it wasn't a good observation of my character,' he said.

'YOUR PITY IS NOTHING, NOT EVEN FOR YOURSELF.'

Zephyrus shook his head and smiled.

'Regret, not pity. There's a difference,' he said.

'REGRET IS FOR THE WEAK.'

Laughter, again. The possession made Mercer lurch towards him with a speed which was more representative of the divine. His fingers clamped around Zephyrus' throat, cutting off his breath as he lifted him off his feet.

'NO MORE TALKING, MEAT. YOU DIE HARD AND HERE.'

Choking, Zephyrus shook in Mercers grasp as he fought to speak.

Mercer tilted his head, the divine consciousness piqued as he lowered Zephyrus and stepped back.

Gagging, Zephyrus tried to squeeze out words, but they were incoherent wheezes until he swallowed and straightened his posture.

'I said, spare me your soliloquy and end this,' he said.

Mercer's face smoothed out as his body shook and, by the cast of his shoulders, became himself again.

He controlled the attendant loss of self, nobility being a perfect frame in which to practice such craft.

'You're right, Zephyrus, time to fulfil your destiny,' he said.

He turned and called for his men.

Then, Podswark by name. He ran into the room, hand on the hilt of his sword, and face tight with focus.

Mercer told him to prepare for the return to the estate. Podswark nodded and left without looking at Zephyrus.

'Even your men see the truth of you, Lord Mercer,' Zephyrus said.

His voice was strained, and to his dismayed experience, inadequate to Phrase anything which would be useful to him.

Mercer smiled and waved him off.

'Yet they obey, which is the truth of power, isn't it?' he said.

Zephyrus shrugged his shoulders.

'Not if the contempt is visible to visitors, but what do I know?' he said.

The strained rasp of his voice lent a harshness which made Mercer's eyes grow wide.

'Very little, which is why I will find more value in you dead than alive,' he said.

Zephyrus sighed and folded his arms.

'I hoped you might have wasted no more of my time,' he said.

Mercer grimaced and spoke before he heard a sharp, metallic sound then a crash of splintering wood.

Zephyrus smiled and watched Mercer as he glanced between him and the sounds of activity outside.

'My men will see to whoever has disturbed us,' he said.

Zephyrus folded his arms then chuckled, despite the tenderness of his throat.

'You should hope they do,' Zephyrus said.

39

Ron decided the Lightning Thesaurus was not an ideal projectile even if he had both arms. However, as a blunt instrument, it was ideal for his needs.

The need to fight armed and trained men with a paralysed arm and a spasmodic gut being of paramount importance to him.

He was slow, accounting for his injuries as he crept to the wall of the fort and crouched, peering around the corner. The stink of burned flesh was thick, coating his sinuses with each breath. There were four men, armed but squatting in a circle, rolling dice. They played in relative silence, the odd cheer or ribald insult aside and so Ron took even more care as he slipped around the corner and dashed behind an outbuilding, made himself as small as possible.

He gauged the distance, acting upon what he hoped was a realistic assessment of his athleticism, and his will to live. Ron took a deep breath, bouncing on his heels then took towards the quartet with the book clamped in his hand. He tucked the spine against his palm, as he drew his good arm back.

They looked up, made siblings by the mutual expression of surprise as Ron ran into the middle of the group, swinging the book in a straight jab forward.

It caught one man on the hinge of his jaw, and he collapsed backwards, the lower half of his face wobbling in a way which nauseated and pleased Ron at the same time. Ron kicked at the man's ankle as he fell, the heel crunching through with enough force to bend it in the opposite direction.

Ron felt a hand on his shoulder and turned, hammering the book into the small bones of his opponent's wrist and then at the elbow in two vicious blows. The man fell away, but then two more pairs of hands grabbed him and Ron's breath leapt from his lungs as a judicious blow slammed into his solar plexus. Ron swung the book out, but it hit air.

He heard the ringing of a drawn blade as another hand pulled the hair on his head hard, lifting his head and he closed his eyes.

Podswark laughed with surprise, three of his men wrestling a child, until he saw the callused, furred feet and the cold yet resigned light in his eyes.

'A halfling?' he said.

One of them was leaning on his side, the foot bent at a nauseating ankle, holding his jaw in place.

Not just any halfling, he thought.

The man with his sword at the halfling's throat looked to Podswark for an order.

Podswark shook his head and the man sheathed his sword with a dissatisfied grunt.

'Bind him and bring him through,' he said.

The men worked with haste, although their roughness was a deliberate way to regain face after the savagery of his assault.

Podswark watched as they picked him up, but he had lapsed into unconsciousness, so they carried his limp form into the fort.

Mercer would be amused to see who had sought to disturb his work. He stopped and looked at the book which had fallen into the dirt. Kneeling down, he picked it up and turned it over in his hands, the runes carved into the leather hummed where his fingertips brushed over them. His eyes narrowed with interest as he stood up, then tucked the book under his arm as he walked after the men and their present for his lord.

Zephyrus saw Ron, bound and unconscious, and hope died in his breast. Ron was pale, damp with dark circles set deep into the flesh under his eyes and his hair clung to his scalp, heavy with sweat.

Two men carried him inside. A suckling pig, Zephyrus thought.

Mercer tittered.

'A child ally?' Mercer said.

Podswark followed them and Zephyrus saw the book under his arm. No, he realised, he felt it. The impact of all those Phrases collated in one space called to him, and he felt a tremor of anticipation and dread.

So close, he thought, *but so was Ron*. Moira, however, was not with them. Questions flew to his lips but then Mercer looked at him.

'You've friends amongst the little folk?' he said

Zephyrus looked at Ron and realised amusement was keeping them both alive.

'He's my apprentice,' he said.

Mercer raised an eyebrow in disbelief.

'A halfling?' he said.

Ron sighed, as his eyelids fluttered.

'He's sick,' the bald man said, as he stepped between the men and Mercer.

'No apprentice though, he fought empty-handed,' he said.

Mercer sneered as he gave a sideways look at Zephyrus.

'Awful choice for a tracker,' Mercer said.

Podswark glanced at Ron then Zephyrus.

'Heard of a halfling like this, empty-handed but something of a reputation,' he said.

Mercer frowned and went over to the halfling, nose wrinkling at the smell wafting from his damp skin.

'For the smell?' he said.

Podswark glanced at him.

'Sick, I reckon, were only using one arm and wielding a bloody book, of all things,' he said.

Mercer smirked as he stared at the halfling.

'Perhaps an apprentice,' he said.

Mercer reached his hand out, asked for Podswark's hatchet, who gave it without speaking.

Zephyrus' heart raced as he put his hand out.

'Please, don't. He's no threat, just a guide, like you said,' Zephyrus said.

Mercer looked at the hatchet then tucked it into his belt.

'Truss the manlet up, we'll take him as a souvenir,' he said.

Podswark gave a tight, shallow bow as he avoided the pleading look in Zephyrus' eyes. He gestured to what had been Zephyrus' cell and the two men took him through.

'We are going home?' Podswark said.

Mercer nodded.

'Better conditions for the ritual,' he said.

Podswark left without speaking. Zephyrus wondered where the man's sympathies laid, but he held his own counsel. Mercer looked at Zephyrus.

'You looked surprised and disappointed, abomination. As am I,' he said.

Zephyrus looked at where they had taken Ron, hearing the sounds of binding, rope coiled and knotted tight around his wrists and ankles, perhaps his neck.

'Amazed you found anyone who follows you,' he said.

Zephyrus smirked.

'I feel that about you, Mercer,' he said.

Mercer blanched as his hand went to the tomahawk on his belt, but then he forced a smile onto his face.

'Go nurse your boy. Then you can tell him how you've failed one another,' he said.

Zephyrus shuffled through to the cell, saw Ron bound on the floor. He was pale, sweating and tattooed with cuts and bruises. His eyes moved beneath the lids, and his breathing was shallow.

Zephyrus knelt down next to him, reached out and found a pulse, stronger than he imagined. Then he felt Ron's face shift as his lips curved into a pained smile.

'Harder to lose a fight than win one,' he said.

Zephyrus put his hand over his mouth.

His mind raced with hopes.

Possibilities.

Fears.

Absences.

A surge of palpable dread.

'Had too many of those,' he said.

Ron turned his head.

'Sometimes the worst fights are the ones you win.'

Zephyrus sneered against his fingers as his eyes widened.

'What happened?'

Ron shifted and rolled onto his back.

'Something there, it took her,' he said.

A stab of pain ran through his gut. He sat up as Zephyrus stepped back.

'Then she took me,' he said.

He rolled his shoulders. Zephyrus noted how his left arm hung down, inert aside from a slow, persistent twitching.

A smile came to him, desperate because he wasn't sure he could do it. Set against it was the slow scream of anguish building inside him.

He wished for the book. Ron's smile softened. He read Zephyrus' expression and looked into his eyes.

'But we got the book,' he said.

40

Zephyrus put a hand out and rested it on Ron's shoulder.

'It cost too much, my friend,' he said.

Ron turned and looked past him through the doorway, into the next chamber.

'You had a look just then,' he said.

Zephyrus closed his eyes.

'An idea, but I don't know, if we could get the book, it would help,' he said.

Ron kept his gaze focused ahead.

'Whatever it is, now would be a fine time to do something with it,' he said.

Zephyrus pressed his fingers against Ron's shoulder. In his head, recalling fragments and theory. The need underneath it all, emotions of grief, urgency, absence, failure and recrimination. Stripped of their names, they were energy. Removed from the context, they were power.

In his head, they came together.

'Viris,' he said.

Ron shuddered as his eyes rolled up in his head and his teeth chattered as his self disappeared for a second. A force reduced and rearranged him with a cold evangelical precision.

A second which felt like an eternity to Ron.

One moment outside himself. Away from pain and grief.

When he returned, still bound but his left arm ached with the dull thump of disuse, over the horrid disconnection between his will and his body.

'Whatever it is, charge a man your weight in gold,' he said.

Zephyrus smiled at the change in his friend.

'All we are, on one level, are impulses and they give us form. Some physicians and linguists, they've made profound observations.'

Ron lifted his hands and touched Zephyrus on the forearm.

'Not now, Sir,' he said.

Zephyrus got up and turned his head. Mercer and his man stood in the doorway.

41

'We shall do this now. I'm hungry,' Mercer said.

Podswark moved into the room. He glanced at his lord, askance as he reached for his sword.

Zephyrus still flush with the success of the application to Ron, raised his head and his teeth crackled, blue sparks spat between them.

'Viri, he said.

Podswarks face slackened. He toppled forwards, cracking against the floor with a sigh of surprised relief as Mercer looked on in disbelief.

A perfect representation of Zephyrus' feelings, seeing how Mercer was unaffected.

'I have my destiny to fulfil, abomination, and it comes to life now,' he said.

Lord Mercer stepped forwards, cradling the axe in his gloved hands as he gave a glacial smile. He seethed with a hateful, incessant hunger.

'Any last words?' he said.

Ron flexed his fingers as he looked at Zephyrus. The dragonborn put back his shoulders and shook his head. He smiled at Ansel.

'Make sure I'm a vicious, terrible monster when you tell people about me,' Zephyrus said.

Ron moved his wrists inside his bonds. There was enough give to allow him to work his way out.

He drove his heels into the ground and stood up. A bolt of pain carved through his head, behind his eyes, but he held his expression. His smile, bloodied and a little crazed, made Ansel blink in disbelief.

'No, Zeph, I want to be the vicious one. Most of his men, they fell at my hands,' he said.

Zephyrus narrowed his eyes as he rocked back, determined to get to his feet. Ansel pointed the axe at him, then Ron, before focusing on Zephyrus again.

'Be still. Die with honour,' he said.

Ron chuckled and shook his head.

'Untie my hands, you bastard,' he said.

Ansel shook his head and drew the tomahawk back toward overhand.

Mercer's aura expanded to embrace the sacrifice to come.

42

Ron kept his gaze fixed with Ansel as he saw the axe blade gleaming in the light.

Ansel barked out a high, broken laugh as Ron fell backwards.

The axe thudded into the wall behind Ron.

Ansel reached for the dagger on his belt, but he couldn't see the petty bastard anywhere. The halfling had moved.

There was the thump of feet against the stone floor, a slow inhalation of breath and the sudden, quiet insistence of an object in motion.

Ansel caught both elbows into the top of his skull, the force concentrated into the points of each. He felt Ron's small, taut legs catch around his throat and although the hilt of his dagger was in his hand, he couldn't make his arm work to wield it.

Ron squeezed, turned his hips, trapping Mercer between his thighs until the building pressure made him collapse and then Ron leapt away. He swung his leg over and tumbled away, landing on his side without getting the breath knocked out of him.

'I would scald the bastard,' Zephyrus said.

Ron chuckled into the floor as he slapped the ground with his palm. When he raised his head, tears streaked his face and made channels through the dirt and blood.

'You shouldn't take pleasure in it, Zephyrus. It's what monsters do,' Ron said.

Zephyrus lowered his jaw and gestured his bound wrists to Ron.

'Gods, too, Ron. Gods, too,' he said.

Ron was a few strides from his friend. Yet as the wounded roar of Mercer reached his ears, he saw the dagger, balanced and already in the air. He was too late to stop Mercer from throwing it.

Ron reached for it, but it was already past his grasp. A bolt of pain stayed his hand as he heard Ansel crow in triumph.

Yet as he clutched at his head, Ron saw the sparks of blue light dance in the air, felt the hum of growing pressure in his sinuses.

Ron turned, his vision distorted by the pain and intensity of Zephyrus calling the lightning.

Everything went white.

Ron felt Zephyrus pick him up. He closed his eyes and sighed as the pressure abated.

'If it helps, I was aiming for the knife,' Zephyrus said.

'Guess. You. Missed,' Ron said.

Zephyrus chuckled as the smoke from Mercer's carbonised corpse trailed into the air.

'One could say that,' Zephyrus said.

Ron wondered if it was a joke but even thinking hurt so he breathed as best he could and thought of nothing at all.

The sounds of alarm, swords being drawn, came to them both. Zephyrus had picked up the book and turned the pages. He looked at Ron and smiled.

'There's a few things I'm keen to try,' he said.

His teeth and eyes blazed blue, snakes of energy which licked at the air with tiny tongues of flame. Ron stepped to one side.

'Who am I to refuse my friend?' he said.

His thoughts turned inward. Saw Moira there, and smiled to her. It was not enough but it would do.

It had to.

Zephyrus walked out of the chamber and spoke to the men.

43
'TWO VISIONS.'

Vivaria was a place wrought with visions and actions which tested the rational.

A peasant in Hanju saw a pebble bloom with flowers. He spoke of nothing else for the rest of his life.

A Midwife, Fionnuala, who had known
students go forth and spread their message
of healing help, felt one pass, but stopped
along the way an iconoclast, after a fashion
but one she thought of with fondness. Now,
concern. She was burning, somewhere.

Two incidents, shared because of some
common factors, came to the interest of
those who held an awareness of such
things.

The estate of Ansel Mercer, in a state of
slow yet certain chaos since his death had a
visitor. He had been there before, but his
appearance was different, and he did not
come alone. A certain amount of
preparation meant this was a different affair
for all parties concerned. He had dressed
for the occasion.

In a suit sixty feet tall and composed of
lightning. He strode towards the estate in
the hours before dawn, firing bright arcs of
blue and white fire into the walls and
buildings, tearing them to pieces like they
were beneath his claws or teeth. The
lightning struck with accuracy and intent,
sparing those with the sense to flee. Most
had but the lightning excised all traces of

Ansel Mercer. It took even the bones of his sacrifices to vapour by the force of his Phrasing.

It took minutes to reduce the buildings to slag, and satisfied, the lightning giant disappeared.

There was another such incident, a week later.

A temple, set into the side of a mountain, stinking with lust and corruption was blessed with a visitor of a lesser divinity, but a purer one.

He sent lightning, shaking the building loose of its foundations, sending brilliant waves of blue and white fire into the stones until they glowed red. The roar of thunder drowned out the screams from within. What disturbed Zephyrus the most, afterwards, was how some screams held the tones of pleasure within them. An ecstasy so intense, it became madness and, he realised, indistinguishable from agony.

They died, all the same.

Keeley was intertwined with a group of cultists, enjoying their blades down her flanks and fingers at her throat when the lightning came. As she burned, in a single flash of incredible heat, she remembered the smile Mercer gave when she undressed in front of him for the first time, and something in her heart reached forwards, a moment too late to grasp its meaning.

It was a strange world, in a strange time, and visions of wonder and horror haunted the minds of many.

Two men, half-dragon and halfling passed the border into Br'ir-Al-Asab, they walked with a mirrored ease, dark from exposure and experience.

The halfling did most of the talking, but he did not speak as a servant to the half-dragon, revered in Br'ir-Al-Asab, but as a herald.

A harbinger.

The sky above them was a clear, brilliant blue as they left the guards behind. There was a bathhouse where they could sit for a time, scrub the stains from their skins, if not their souls, and then get down to business.

Ron wanted to renegotiate his contract.

THE END.